Praise for *This Other Salt*

'Hussein's stories are about in
exile, where the world itself is
moving and highly aesthetic ex

'Whether he is writing of Java, Pakistan or London, his writing, uniquely his own, many-layered and full of references and allusions, imbued with the music of the Gamelan and Persian and Urdu poetry, crosses continents.' **Shena McKay**

'A canvas of memories, divided by borders, political and human ... they evoke the moods of a past left behind, a restlessness with the present, and the displacement caused by migration in the post-colonial world.' *Literary Review*

'Beautifully written and tinged with sadness, these stories are a treat for readers.' *Newsline*

'*This Other Salt* will add to the richness and density of writings in English, and help the reader traverse different cultures.' *Wasafiri*

'The symbolic and intellectual complexity of Hussein's collection is undeniable.' *TLS*

'Each story, remarkable in both expansiveness and precision, sings with heartbreak, intelligence and elegy. A stunning collection.' **Kamila Shamsie**

'A book that I would keep for a rainy day, that seems to demand the concentrated attention to reading that a heavy monsoon shower can bring in its wake.' *Biblio*

'Hussein is perfectly at home with the multi-cultural realities of our metropolitan life. His linguistic resources, his lucid, luminous prose, make the act of cultural negotiation both a discovery and a revelation.' *The Book Review*

Also by the Author

This Other Salt

Hoops of Fire

Mirror to the Sun

Aamer Hussein

TURQUOISE

Saqi Books

British Library Cataloguing-in-Publication Data
A catalogue record for this book is available from the
British Library

ISBN 0 86356 325 2

First published 2002 by Saqi Books

Saqi Books
26 Westbourne Grove
London W2 5RH
www.saqibooks.com

Contents

Cactus Town

He brought me white roses,
White muscat roses,
And asked me gently: May I
Sit with you on the rock?

Anna Akhmatova

1

He fell in love with Nuria when he saw her walking on fire. Live coals had been laid out on parched summer grass and she walked over them faster than the other virgins. He wasn't supposed to be there but he was watching from his place behind an almond tree. She crossed the burning ember field and fainted.

Sakina was thirsty. Abbas went out to look for water and they riddled him with arrows. Kasim the bridegroom was shot down on his wedding night. Hussein's horse returned sand-matted and blood-soaked without his master.

All day long the desert wind blows. Birds fall to the ground. On the tenth night of Muharram blood streaks the sky. He weeps for them all and his eyes are red but he never wept as bitterly as he did for Nuria.

2

Aunty Mehri tried to grow all kinds of flowers in her garden. Hydrangea, hibiscus, black rose. But everything withered there. Only wild flowers kept blooming and cactus thrived. It's the desert, she said. The salt and the sandy wind kill plants in this town. But in Chand's garden, you could see blossoms of every colour, finely trimmed hedges, fruit trees heavy with green mangoes and papayas.

Aunty Mehri – Begum Meher Taj Shah – was Nuria's aunt, not really ours. She was the widow of our great-uncle, who'd been killed by the Japs in Malaya in 1944 when she was thirty-two. We knew him as the Picture on the Wall. On holidays, her family visited his tomb with flowers and incense as if he were a saint. She had three children: her daughter was with her husband in our embassy in China, her son Tahir had a house across the the lane from us, and her youngest son Mahir, the light of her eyes, was studying in England: he only came home in summer. Mehri lived in a turreted mansion her husband had built in the thirties, in the old part of town by the sea. We called it Cactus Town. A lover came to visit her now and then, from Rawalpindi where he kept his wife.

Mehri was tall and pale with lacquered short dark hair. She dressed in black chiffon at night and in white lace with matching gloves and scarves in daylight. Every few weeks she swooped across town to visit us; we knew she wanted Tahir's wife to see her arrive. Ten years ago she'd looked for a bride for her son among the daughters of her own patrician family in Hyderabad Deccan, but she settled instead on her husband's niece, seventeen-year-old Nazar Zahra, and changed her name to Chand because her face was bright as the moon. Mehri had hoped that Chand's big dowry would be the making of Tahir. But Chand's great misfortune was that she'd married a man who loved good whisky more than he loved his marriage bed. The docile girl turned into a lazy woman. Much to her mother-in-law's chagrin, she'd rise at midday and play mahjong all afternoon. In the evenings you could see her walking alone in her garden, up and down and up again, prayer beads in her hand, waiting for her husband to come home, but he never came home until after midnight, when we'd wake up from our dreams and hear the powerful engine of his car roar up our lane and the black iron gates shut behind him.

3

On Sundays we play by the lakes. There are two lakes, one blue, one green. They call the green one the Maneater: it claims a few people each year. They say ill-starred lovers and ill-treated wives go there to give it their lives. We play by the blue one, or get in ear-deep though we're not allowed to; we're not afraid of typhoid or diphtheria.

My name is Kamran. I'm nine. I have grey eyes and very dark skin. Nuria comes here with her cousin's children, Mahnur, who's my age, and Mehriyar who's eight; they're my cousins too. Sometimes Abbas, Chand's brother, who's thirteen, brings them to play. Nuria is eleven. She sits on the grassy bank, braids flowers into garlands, and sings:

I'm off to chase shadows of echoes
in the country where butterflies sing

— Snaggletooth, raggyhair, snotpicker, stinkbomb, elephantfoot, who's going to marry you, Nuria?

– I'll marry Nuria.

– Hey, dress up the bridegroom, here comes his elephant, dress him in gold.

They rub dust in my face. And in Nuria's hair. They push Nuria into water. I follow. Pebbles, like marble, washed sky-smooth beneath our feet.

4

Meher Taj had once had a brother. Everyone thought Alezamin was dead. But truth to tell he'd simply disappeared. He'd left behind a wife and a son and a daughter. His grass widow was a hapless thin creature with straw-coloured hair and staring great eyes. We heard she'd been a Hindu whose family had deserted her when they went over the border. Aunty Mehri, who was working then with destitute women as she now worked with unwanted children, had found her in a camp and, when she said she had nowhere to go, had taken her home as a kind of superior servant because she seemed educated. She renamed her Sadia. Alezamin, who'd recently arrived from Hyderabad, had seen her at Mehri's and immediately fallen in love. He'd married her against Mehri's wishes.

Many years later, soon after he disappeared one night, Sadia came to Mehri's door for help: she said she'd found work in an airline office, and she'd sent her son to a boys school as a weekly boarder, but she wanted someone to take in her daughter. She couldn't make enough to feed herself and two.

No one could understand why Aunty Mehri refused to take in the child. She lived alone and could have done with a little girl's company. No one could understand, either, why after refusing to help Sadia, she told her – almost as an afterthought – to visit Chand. Because Mehri and Chand had cordially detested each other since mother-in-law had forced daughter-in-law to abort her third child which was, she claimed, the result of Chand's wanton interlude with a passing lover. And Chand had pleaded with Tahir to take her away from his mother's kingdom; they'd live in the house she had built on the other side of town.

Chand took in Sadia's daughter, and brought her up with her own children Mahnur and Mehriyar. The girl stayed in the shadows, helped with minor chores, and went to a charity school down the road where she was taught to sew, cook and keep accounts in beautiful handwriting.

And when she came home, the luminous name her father had given her, Nurafshan, Light-sprinkler, had somehow become Nuria.

5

– Can you really hear the butterflies singing, Nuria?

   – Sometimes.

   – How far can you follow an echo, Nuria?

   – As far as your breath takes you.

   – Will you marry me when we're big?

   – Silly boy. Wait and see.

   – Please?

   – If you want me to I will.

6

At the seashore. Nuria sits on moist whitish sand with her toes in water and watches the spray rise. She listens to the sea singing. She thinks it brings her messages, written in foam on the waves. The sea tells her a bridegroom will come for her, his face covered in flowers. Gold so heavy on her body she'll faint. Her feet bathed in milk. The Five Blessed Ones will bless her wedding. She'll wake every morning in a bed of silver.

I bring her translucent shells, dead starfish, and a conch which, when she puts it to her ear in her bed at night, will sing her the sea's songs.

Far away, etched against the grey horizon, there's a single red, blue and yellow sail.

Aunt Chand has a fat Iraqi friend named Farkhanda who can tell fortunes from tea leaves and coffee grounds. There's no sun today, but May is so hot that even the sea's on the boil and we're close to wishing we weren't here. The ladies lie on deck chairs, smoking menthol cigarettes, mugs of coffee sweetened with condensed milk beside them. Farkhanda calls to Nuria, who's lost in her dreams of what the sea will bring her:

— Come, child, let me tell you who you'll marry.

And Chand, in imitation of her children, says:

— Who'll marry Nuria, she's so plain...

— Plain? She's stunning, Farkhanda says, looking at tall Nuria's fifteen years. Come and sit down here and give me your hand. Yes, I see a tall dark man, with a gun in his hand, who fights to save his land, a brave soldier...

— Don't put silly ideas in the child's head, Chand says.

But then... I can tell you what happens, I am watching, just surfacing from the waves:

A great big car with windows curtained in black drove up to our hut. The tall man who was driving leapt out to open a door. Aunty Mehri emerged from a cocoon of lemon-scented airconditioning, immaculate and cool as always in lilac georgette. She took the youth's arm and came up to us.

– I didn't know you'd be using our hut today, she said to her daughter- in-law. Her tone was faintly venomous, her smile lopsided. But Chand wasn't listening. She'd stood up to fling her lovely white arms around the dark neck of her young brother-in-law, Mahir. He lifts her off the sands, swings her round, and then, as they laughingly disengage, I see Nuria's face, her lips parted and trembling, her teeth shine, her lashes throw shadows on her cheek. She's in a trance; she seems to be praying.

7

– Where can you hear a butterfly's song, Nuria?

   – Silly boy. How can I tell?

   – How long is the shadow of an echo, Nuria?

   – As long as the nose on your idiot face.

   – So you won't marry me, Nuria?

   – Didn't you hear what Khala Farkhanda said? I'm going to marry a fighting man with a gun.

   – I'll become a hero for your sake. I'll get a gun.

   – Silly.

   – Give me back my starfish and my shells.

8

At seventeen Nuria, oiled braids hanging down her back and crushed dull cotton clothes, becomes voluptuous. She spends her spare hours reading bright-covered romances about girls called Naela and Romana; orphaned, or separated from their families at Partition, they cry a lot in corners for cousins who fight for their land and their nation.

Mahir's married now, to a girl from Ilford. He met her when he was on holiday, in her father's pub where she worked. He brings her home to meet the family. Her name's Brenda; it's obvious their child will be what we call a seven-month baby. Mehri meets her with icy courtesy, but we've been briefed: kindness to Brenda amounts to letting down the side. If we do talk to her, we should make her feel like a Martian, a freak from a travelling carnival.

Wrapped in a colourful cheap nylon sari she's been given by Mehri, Cockney vowels and glottals contending valiantly with multisyllabic names, freckles riotous and skin reddening in the June desert sun, Brenda looks, poor girl, outlandish. We're sure it won't last; Mahir's exploits in town, before he left, were legendary; he'd been sent away, in haste, after two beatings by friends whose girls he'd stolen, and a murder threat from a betrayed husband. We hear that Mehri has offered her the pot of gold at the end of the rainbow if only she'll run off to get it, back to Ilford, maybe, where Mehri implies Brenda can open her own nice pub with her takings. But Brenda is a barmaid with a pot of gold for a heart. She'd wanted to please her redoubtable mother-in-law when she first came here, but now she's rolling up absent sleeves to fight for her hero.

Soon Mahir and Brenda are far, far away from us, back in England; living, we hear, in Essex, from where, with his Cambridge education, Mahir commutes to his job as a chartered accountant in Leadenhall Street.

9

This season we're all in love with love. We've put away our James Taylor and our Melanie records; we're listening, instead, to Tahira Syed singing 'Abhi to main jawan hun', we're reciting verses by Faiz. It's our last year here before we leave for foreign universities; Mahnur will read philosophy at Cambridge, Mehriyar is going to the London School of Economics, and my father wants me to study law. As for Nuria, she'll stay behind with Chand: she wants to be a dressmaker.

The white moonflower, with its many petals, blooms from its cactus-like vine on our white wall and Mehri descends on the house to look at it. Hanging overhead, there's a huge red moon like a lantern; it's supposed to be so bright you can read by it. Nuria, in white like a Chughtai painting, comes to the garden with rose sherbet, rock candy and milky sweets on a silver tray decorated with frangipani; she's in competition with the white flowers and the fiery moon. Mehri, who's never yet had a smile or a blessing for her, is looking her over tonight like a buyer in a cattle market selecting a calf.

Then, when the long fasting season has whittled down the moon to a sliver of silver, Chand's brother Abbas comes over from his military academy, in time for the big Eid. He whistles film tunes and wears tight bright shirts with enormous collars and flared trousers that flap as he jumps off his motorbike. His hair is short, because he's a soldier, but he's hung up his uniform for now.

One look at Nuria dressed up in Chand's opulent castoffs, her brown hair and golden skin and wide hips, and longing soaks him in sweat. He's pined for her since he saw her fainting after she walked on fire last Muharram.

– She seems like a homeloving girl, Abbas says. I bet she can cook.

– She's a comfort to me, Chand responds. Another daughter. A bit moody sometimes. Yes, of course she can. Cook, I mean.

– Is she spoken for? I wondered if...

We'd thought Chand might act as Mehri does about her men,

but no: she tells her brother to wait a year or two to be married
— they're both so young, he's waiting for his commission, and
in any case long engagements are appropriate But come back,
she says, in a month or two, with a ring. Nuria, when asked
for her consent, nods wordlessly, brown eyes fixed on hennaed
toes. Abbas brings her a ruby ring. The more unkind among
the neighbours say: When he looks at his young cousin Nuria,
the sleeping tiger awakens in Tahir's eye. And Chand is afraid
of a rival.

Nuria begins to prepare her trousseau. Quiet, dull as usual
in company, she stitches sequins on scarves, brocade on hems,
embroiders endless flower patterns on napkins and
pillowcases. She says her prayers three times a day. Abbas is
heir to a fortune; we tell her she'll become a fat bejewelled
landowner's darling in two years.

When Farkhanda comes to visit and asks if Abbas — so
gentle and mild — is what Nuria really wants, the girl replies:

— It's Chand Bhabi's wish. Since she's always done so much
for me, it's probably God's will. And you told me I'd marry a
soldier.

10

— Where's your soldier gone, O Nuria, where's your soldier
gone, far, far away...

– Guess what I'm doing, Kami.

– What, Nuria?

– I'm listening to the butterflies singing. I think I heard the echo of a shadow. Want to come with me to look?

– Where can you ever hear butterflies singing, Nuria? That's kid's stuff.

11

Nuria was to marry Abbas in November. But suddenly Aunty Meher Taj heard the call of blood and binding family ties.

– My beloved brother's daughter, after all, she said, waving her Sobranie. Only I can give her away as a bride. This is her home, I'm her closest surviving relative.

Sadia, of course, she'd forgotten. But it did appear strange that the bride-to-be should be sleeping under the same roof as her fiance. So Chand, saying she didn't want to burden poor Sadia who lived in the distant suburb of North Nazimabad which none of us had had the misfortune of visiting, reluctantly agreed. Nuria packed all her bags and was driven across town from Hill Park to Clifton to live in her aunt's seaside palace. We couldn't imagine her, so far away from Chand, in distant Cactus Town.

We didn't see her again till the smaller Eid. Mahir had come home on holiday from Ilford without his unloved wife, biting the bit after three or four years of suburban bliss. Handsome as ever, hair in waves to his shoulders. purple velvet jacket thrown over his arm, he delighted us with stories of swinging London. He'd driven Nuria over, with Mehri, for our biannual lunch, an occasion for family rituals and reconciliations. Nuria was transformed. Gold-streaked hair, artfully loosened from its braid, framed a painted face. Her eyes and even her lashes were tinted with turquoise kohl to match the transparent turquoise chiffon that swathed her, leaving inches of glowing shoulder and midriff on view.

– What have you done to yourself, Chand hissed. You look like a tart.

And Mahir looked like a man entranced.

Desire and youth have done what Mehri's money and wiles couldn't. There are, as usual, as many tales as there are heads to tell them. Everyone knows and the news travels down to our lane from the sea: handsome Mahir has given his heart to his beautiful cousin Nurafshan. They're all over town, at hotels, at the swimming pool, in the countryside, at the beach. Shameless, some say. An orphan who only just got engaged to a soldier. So what if Mahir's ten years older? say others. He's still only twenty-eight. A whole life ahead of him. It's only right, it's the way it should always have been, he's going to leave his cheap slut of a foreign wife and come home to settle down with his maternal uncle's daughter.

We don't know how Abbas finds out: perhaps Nuria phones him, or writes, in her elegant script and stilted English, that she can't marry him, life changed her plans; she's sorry for breaking her word, but what can she do? She can't live a lie. But Abbas won't tell, won't hear a word against her, and we're on Chand's side, not talking to Mahir or Nuria.

Chand, when she hears, drives down to Mehri's villa. She's surprisingly calm. She claims she knows what the old dragon's up to; using her orphaned niece as bait, to tempt her beloved son away from his foreign wife. She's not going to stand back and watch. Nuria thinks life is a romance by Razia Butt, does she? She'll think again when, all too soon, she sees Mahir's departing back. Nuria, and Mehri, can keep the gifts that Chand had given; all she wants for her brother is the engagement ring, which was reset from melted gold and a ruby left him by their mother. But what had Abbas done to deserve this? And how, she demands, will Nuria ever repay her for so many years of love? After all, blood was thicker than water, and there was no tie of blood to bind her to Nuria.

12

When Chand took back the ring to her brother, Abbas said:
   – You should have left it to me. I'd have made her see the light. She'll never be happy with that swine.
   He put the ring in his pocket and took off on his motorbike. He didn't come back that day.
   – When he came home, Chand told us, he said he'd seen Nuria, though he didn't say where. Then he wept like I've never seen him weep before. Every year at the processions he flays his chest till he draws drops of blood for the love of Hussein and Abbas and Kasim and sometimes he even uses little knives but this time the blood seemed to flow from his eyes.

13

Abel and Cain – the war has fallen on our necks like those fighting brothers and one of them will have to die. Shiploads of boys transported across land and sea to fight, to keep a country they've never seen, for the glory of a nation split at birth. Abbas is out east already, by the Burma border. He's in a guerilla-breaking squadron. Chand says: Why are we sending our sons and brothers across enemy territory to stop foreigners from speaking their own language and a strange faraway land from changing its name?

Karb o bala. Agony and affliction.

News from the frontlines is bad, then worse.

14

The telegram came at night:

WE HAVE THE HONOUR MADAME TO
ANNOUNCE THE GLORIOUS MARTYRDOM IN
ARMED COMBAT OF YOUR BROTHER
LIEUTENANT SAYYAD ABBAS HAIDAR

And Chand didn't act, as we'd expected, like a hero's sister, with dignity, in silence. She tore her hair and her clothes and beat her breast, she threw herself on the floor, and she didn't have to say a word, but we knew that in her heart she was cursing the leaders and the war, and cursing Nuria, again and again, for bringing bad luck to her beloved dead brother.

And my eyes are no longer grey.

15

And Nuria: when she heard the news they say she bent and smashed her green and red glass bangles on the stones. She spent three nights in her room, praying. She didn't even leave a message for Mahir when on the third day she walked away from her aunt's house, leaving Cactus Town where flowers wouldn't grow. She never turned back. She stepped out in the clothes she'd had on since her morning shower and walked alone in Clifton until she found a rickshaw by the old shrine. Chand's house was full of mourners that day, but it wasn't from Chand she sought asylum: she knew she no longer had a home there, and after all there were no blood ties to take her to the house of mourning. She went back to her mother and brother, to the life she'd left nine years before, the shabby flat, the city's outskirts. Some say she was pregnant and the first child she gave her husband was Mahir's son. Others said she was made, like Chand all those years ago, to have an abortion. She accepted the first proposal she got. A few weeks later she was married off, we heard, to an aging widower her mother had found in the matrimonial columns, with several children of his own: the number reported varies according to the teller. None of us attended the wedding but some sent gifts. Mahir went back to his wife in Ilford, where he lived for many years, until Brenda, keeping their money and their growing daughters, threw him out, and he flew back across the sea to live with Meher Taj. He gave up accountancy and turned Cactus Town into a tutorial college. Chand, Mahnur and Mehriyar never spoke to Nuria again, not even when Chand, at barely forty, died of a terrible flowering in her brain.

Mehri, too, chose silence. We heard, years later, that Nuria's husband kept her jewellery and sent her back to her mother. She had some hard years after that, bringing up two children alone.

16

But when I told my sister I was writing this story she remembered:

Ten years ago. An April afternoon. A hand touched her shoulder on the lawn of the Sind club where she was running after her three-year-old daughter. She turned around to see a woman in her late thirties, elegant, blonde and discreetly bejewelled. Don't you recognise me? she asked. I'm your cousin. Nurafshan... Nuria. They kissed. Before her chauffeur-driven car came up the gravelled drive she introduced my sister to her husband, a handsome man slightly older than her. As many tales as there are heads to tell them. He wasn't a widower, only divorced; he spent a lot of time in Dubai, but he'd never sent her away.

And later, when she thought about it, my sister wondered who it was that Nuria had begun to remind her of.

17

Sometimes I dream I'm in Abbas's place: I'm the one Nuria turns down. She comes up to me, face ashy with tears, kneels in the garden, takes my hands in hers, asks her childhood friend to forgive her, to remain her friend. She places my hands against her damp cheeks. She reminds me of butterfly songs and echoes and shadows. But I'm a sea rock; I turn my face away. Forgive me Nuria, I say in silence, I don't understand these things, I'm too young, I can't be your friend any more. Then I ride off into the night on my motorbike, ride it right to the edge of the sea, leave it there and walk into the waves.

That's how the policemen, when they find it, know where to look for Abbas, and when fishermen haul his body up from the sea days later his face has been disfigured by crabs. Nuria's ruby ring is still buttoned into his pocket. But that's another version, in which Abbas never went to war: he wouldn't have understood what he was fighting for, why he should give his life to stop a strange country from breaking away or changing its name and keeping its language.

Too grey an ending for me. I'm a teller of stories. I want to dip my finger in a war wound and spell the name of a hero. I have no time for an insignificant boy who mourns lost loves and gives his life to the sea. So why is salt water seeping through this page?

Electric Shadows

Don't think I haven't changed. Who said
absence makes the heart grow fonder?
Though I watch the sunset redden
every day, days don't grow longer.

Mimi Khalvati, 'Don't Ask me, Love, for
that First Love' (after Faiz Ahmed Faiz)

ACT I

Night Music

This I remember of the rest of '65:

Dining in a garden of light. We had picked fallen frangipani, jasmine and hibiscus from grass. They'd lie in crystal swans and silver boats that night. Garlands of red, green and yellow bulbs were intertwined with branches of tall trees. It was a holiday, Easter probably, because we hadn't gone to school. I turned ten that day, though my birthday had been celebrated, along with my younger sister's, ten days before. Tonight's invitation read:

> *To bid farewell to HE the Ambassador of Belgium*
> *Nawabzada and Begum A... H...*
> *Request the pleasure of your company for dinner*
> *at 8 pm*
> *on 8.4.1965*
> *at 43/4/B-Block 6*
> *P.E.C.H.S.*

When we went in after dinner, the American Ambassador's daughter Drusilla sang Dylan's songs on her guitar. Then my mother, dressed in white edged with old rose and gold, performed selections from her repertoire of traditional songs. The sounds of sarangi haunted the air.

Planting corn and petunias. There were flowers everywhere, black roses, orchids, bluebells, orange blossom, hydrangea, hibiscus. And things you could eat. Black wild berries beneath clusters of pink and yellow flowers. The sweet-sour flesh of almond, crack the reached shell for the nut. Corn cobs wih their long flaxen tresses. Green coconuts for sweet water. Some flowers have stems you can suck honey from. Then there's the bitter hard fruit they call caronda, radish red concealing white unripe but it ripens to deep red and it bleeds, you can pretend you're wounded, you can cry.

Beaches. Ochre or white, in light and shadow. Bubbly blue transparent creatures cling to your calf, their sting sharper than a bee's bite. Starfish, I think, are dead, purplish hard bodies more strangely structured than a star. Crabs scuttle by. The smell of camels, like rain-washed dogs. Sand flecked with glittering mica, so hot beneath my soles I can't get my swollen feet into my black suede shoes. They say there are sharks further out to sea, they tell us to beware: we can't swim and deeper in the water there are shelves. Sand slips from under your feet. The waves will carry you away. My sister Safinaz and I hold hands when we walk in. Waves lash out and we jump. But for a moment, we let them engulf us, for the terror, for the thrill.

Night falling. Musicians pass our lane in threes or fours.

Playing drums and pipes and strings. Their voices tough and torn and tender, they sing: *pere pavandisan chavandisan*, they sing: *mor tho tilley rana*, they sing: *o man ghure mushtaq san*. The songs of Sohni and Momal and Sassi of Bambor. Words and yearnings we don't understand. But we run to the gate to listen. They drag bicycles behind them.

I think the locust swarm came that year and ate up the saplings in the garden. The gardener cried. No, I'm turning the calendar's pages too fast: that'll come later.

The Canadian Cat

Then there was Madeline. From Ottawa. Her hair was yellow, streaked bright and dark, thick, with the rippling look that women, in later years, will pay to achieve. Her fringe fell into grey-green eyes. She wasn't pretty; her nose was flattish and broad. But she had a wide smile and tan-gold skin. I didn't choose her for myself: I doubt I would have. The three other boys and twenty-odd girls in class, for once in unison, did it for me. They paired us off. Every day, they'd wait for us at recess and grab us in the cloak room where we went to get our sandwich boxes, push us into each other, knock our heads together, so that in our attempts to escape them and each other we'd be intertwined for moments at a time, arms and legs and eyes and breath, before the bell rang and we got away.

Madeline Weld. We were in the same class at the Convent of Jesus and Mary. In that last year before the capital moved from Karachi to Islamabad, carrying away its cosmopolitan crowd. Most of the foreign boys had already gone. My friends from last term, Raoul Severe and Tommy Kanhai, had left one after the other, for Florida and Japan. Norwegian Helen, who spoke Urdu better than I did, had long since chosen to observe unwritten protocols of segregation and a new deskmate, while I, one of only four boys who stayed on for those final months of co-education, sat with Ashley, Mark and Jamil in the male enclave.

I don't know how long the bullying lasted, and I don't think it had started before the summer holidays, because I couldn't have borne that sixty-day break without seeing Madeline. But maybe I did and maybe I learned then that waiting, and dreaming alone, had as much of a charge as the closeness of someone you love.

You will want me to tell you about the city and the time, paint the house on the hill and the place where we lived. And of course I should mention the poor, who the nuns say are always with us, but they're half a mile away from my lane and my life. Linger with me, instead, where the light falls. Breathe in the fragrance of freshly cut grass. Taste the tartness of unripe mango on my tongue.

So let's say it all started after the summer break, in August, when we came back to school. Those cloakroom encounters went on for three weeks – or six? Then I went to Mrs Evans, our Welsh class teacher, and complained. The children were reprimanded and I was up in everybody's esteem, for having had the courage to protest. I don't know what Madeline felt.

The first break from her must have been during Michaelmas. I'd persuaded my parents to let me have a white lamb. I called her Snowy. She followed me everywhere I went. We'd always had dogs in the yard, and my sisters kept Lena, a dachschund, in their room, so we'd all go for a walk to the ponds together, children, lamb and dog.

Our house was far from the sea, the marshes and their fetid fishy smell. But there were two ponds half a mile away. One was green and smelly. The other, blue and clear with foliage and wildflowers around: we bathed in it. Near the ponds was a house we'd stroll past. I thought it was Madeline's because I'd seen a pale-coffee Dodge with a CD number plate, like the one that carried her away from school, sail down its drive. But then someone told me she lived in Clifton, close to school and the sea, miles away, not near me or the ponds at all.

But that I found out later, when my new confidence gained me new friends. The best of these was thirteen-year-old Tina. (Years later, she'd write a confessional memoir that was a success and a scandal.) She sat next to me during our Urdu lesson when Madeline and the other foreigners left our classroom to study French verbs next door. Tina'd had to drop out of school for two years or more because she'd been ill, with meningitis, I think. She wasn't good at her studies but had instead that peculiar quality so lacking in most of us: you could, I suppose, call it gaiety, combined with her brand of peasant chic. Her skin, hair and eyes were all the colour of amber. Tina and I spent breaks together. Since she had a throng of admirers, among whom were the toughest girls in school, no one dared to tease me about her the way they'd ragged me about Madeline, though this was real and that an invention, and I suppose Tina treated me a bit like a brother.

Tina and our friends had borrowed a trend current among seniors for years, a sort of friendship album called a slambook, in which each page began with a question. They ranged from the simplest: Where do you live? to the more provocative: Whom would you choose to kiss on the beach? Your friends were compelled to answer with wit and wisdom. With Tina's help, and lots of responses from her friends, I presented the class with a perfected literary version of myself, the first ever. I was feisty, wise-cracking, I had a life outside school as wayward as a kite on the breeze, I had friends among older girls (true) and listened to the best music (also true, because, courtesy of my sisters, I was singing Francoise Hardy in cod French).

Madeline had a best friend called Fiona Campbell, with frizzy ginger hair and freckles and a Scottish accent, who asked to fill in my slam-book and when it came back to me Madeline had given as much information about herself as I could possibly deal with, including her phone number, which was 51112. It was the first sign that she actually did like me. But there were revelations to follow. Below one of Tina's more inventive questions, Madeline had written:

> *For Aamer:*
> *I am a cabbage*
> *Divide me in two*
> *My leaves I give to others*
> *My heart I give to you*

Madeline had been brave enough in her own way to respond to my ruse to gain her attention and extract information about her with a clumsy message of love.

The Child Jesus and the Green Man of the River

Was that before, or after, the war?

That spat between neighbours started in September. At school it was cause for excitement, particularly for us Pakistani children, who had only a short while before refused to attend Catholic prayers and now had a room of our own to start the day where we sang the national anthem instead of the Lord's Prayer.

Safinaz and I had been told by our mother that God was light, He was everywhere, within and without, and I'd read that our Prophet was a man who said he was like other men and less than perfect, only chosen as a messenger by God. But at the Convent the nun's God, at once Father, Son, and Messiah, was a personification, with bleeding alabaster wounds. Easy with our own domestic faith, I didn't like Catholicism, found it guilt-ridden and scary. Latin hymns sung in chorus reminded me of horror movies. I didn't like our Sister Superior, Maria Gheratti. And she didn't like me. She'd find any excuse to rap my palms and my soles with her lethal ruler. (Later, when I was just about to leave school, I interrupted a conversation the tough girls in class were having about fast girls and boyfriends to add: The Bible is full of prostitutes. Jezebel, Mary Magdalen. And Salome who sold herself to her stepfather in exchange for John the Baptist's head. I'd seen that in 'King of Kings' in Bombay the year before. Karachi didn't allow personifications of holy prophets on film in public places. I felt Ma. Gheratti's hand descend like an axe on the nape of my neck. She must have said, as she always did: the child Jesus weeps when you sin. It's the sick bay for you. Soap and water for your dirty tongue. I'd wonder how Jesus, who'd died, we were told, at thirty-three, had reverted to infancy after the crucifixion. By then, almost in pursuit of Ma. Gheratti's persecution, I'd become the only rebellious boy in class, the resident clown, acting out others' fantasies. I delighted in being thrown out of the classroom, and making the children laugh by pulling faces or dancing in the doorway.)

At home, my companion, close as a twin, was still Safinaz. Our bond was mostly wordless. The best friend we shared was Mehreen. Six months older than me, she was strong and lovely, with silky brown hair and a tough, street-wise manner which saw us through all the hazards of childhood. If you came looking for us before sunset you'd find us three on the rocky steps of the pavilion at the back of the house by the hibiscus tree, seeing who could jump off the highest peak. (Lithe Safinaz, the smallest, was always the winner.) For a season or two we played croquet on the lawn, until the smell of Mother's baking drew us indoors for shortbread, elephant's ears, tarts, even, sometimes, a pizza. Oftener still, we'd be elbow-deep in mud with no care for the afternoon sun, building forts, baking our backs and faces. Or we'd be following my sister Shahrukh down the stony paths of hills further away, filling vases and jars with tadpoles which soon became frogs that she'd throw back into stagnant water. (She loved beasts, my sister Shah. Once she rescued a donkey from a man who was beating it, telling him, to his amazement, that she'd take him to the Society for Prevention of Cruelty to Animals. When finally someone came to our gate and led it to some other grim pasture, she spent hours imitating it bray.)

Mehreen took me in hand. It must have been during the war. We'd been told not to come to school because there were rioters on the streets; the nuns thought they were likely to attack cars with diplomatic number plates. Then Mehreen dialled 51112. We listened on extensions. After asking for Madeline, we called her, in a chorus of fake American accents, Mad Madeline, Ottawa owl, Canadian Cat, and Ontario Idiot. All poor Madeline said was: Is this some kind of joke?

Another afternoon, Mehreen, hair set with beer and arranged in a shining waterfall, came with us to our exhibition of paintings at school and I noticed Madeline, awe in her eyes, staring.

Was that before, or after, the war?

It was said that Madame Noor Jehan the Melody Queen, the country's most famous singer who'd once been a movie star, had gone to the radio station on the first day of war with a sheaf of lyrics in praise of our soldiers and pilots and sailors tucked under an ample arm. She'd set them to music right there, demanding they be recorded on the spot. Her songs filled the airwaves – *Ai watan ke sajile javano, merya dhol sipaiya* – and we sang them all day, even at school, but the nuns didn't say a word. We wondered whose side they thought the Child Jesus was on.

When we came home we'd have to draw the curtains at sundown and make sure not a ray of light escaped. There were blackouts and sirens all evening and on the radio the resonant tones of newscaster Shakeel Ahmed would tell of General Musa and the valiant exploits of our boys at the border. There were also tales of how Khizr in the form of Darya Pir, the green man of the river Indus, had led soldiers out of trouble or into battle. And for days people stood in their gardens for a glimpse of the comet they'd been told was flashing in the sky: Zulfikar, they said, the sword of Ali himself, a symbol of the victory we'd soon be celebrating.

At home Safinaz and I played Indian and Pakistani soldiers. The carpet was India, the sofas, divans and window ledges were Pakistan. Pakistan, of course, won every time, but Safinaz and I would fight about our roles: who'd play the enemy, who the valiant soldier.

Being sent home during the last three or four days of war meant being without Tina and Ashley and Mark and Jamil and all the rest. Worse, it meant not seeing Madeline.

When ceasefire was declared, people on the streets went mad: they set fire to the United States Information Centre, where we went to borrow books, because they held America responsible for Pakistan's decision, considered cowardly, to abandon the war. I wonder what Karachi's resident foreigners felt about the fighting. Their own great war was, after all, twenty years behind them; but the Americans were involved at the time in a fierce combat, in distant Vietnam. Madeline, though she was Canadian, belonged to a group that must have felt at least mildly anxious, in a city where all whites looked the same to the natives.

Mother's American friend Genevieve had got off her ship at Karachi and spent a day with us, earlier that year, on her way to Vietnam. She was going there to look for her son; he was twenty-five, had been drafted and was now Classified Missing. His Mormon wife, convinced he was dead, wanted to remarry. His mother was sure he was still alive.

Throughout the war Daddy had been stranded in Bombay, where our mother's sister lived. He'd stopped there on his way back from Ceylon, little knowing that war would be declared when he landed. His family and friends had to break curfew to see him there. He couldn't get in touch with us for those three weeks, though Bombay was less than an hour's flight away. We had to be sure he was safe. We never dared to think he might go missing too. We'd been too busy to worry, with our celebrations of victory, our war games, our glamorous president Ayub. Until we got tired of warfare and generals.

Now the war was over: Daddy was coming home. He called from Beirut. He'd been able to fly there as soon as they let foreigners leave Bombay. He'd be back as soon as he'd got us some gifts. Our gaudy rag dolls, which we'd bought from some market on the Rajasthan border on holiday in India, were dancing on the day he came back to a melody we'd composed, sung in gipsy voices, inspired by the songs the passing night musicians play, with a lyric we'd written ourselves.

The Eve of St Agnes

Daddy's gifts: great balls of salty-sour Dutch cheese in red waxed paper, white chocolate which we took to school to share with friends, and magic slates – all you had to do was write or draw on a waxy sheet and lift it off the black slate surface below when you were tired of what you'd written or drawn.

One day I left my slate behind in the big room we called our study. One of our sisters – Yasmine, I seem to remember, though she didn't have much time for us – came to play table tennis there with Mehreen's brother Zeyn, her best friend. She picked it up, probably to scribble a score on it. Engraved in the sticky black, where their traces remained after the paper on which they'd been written had been lifted off to erase them, she saw the letters that spell Madeline's name. In fact, she may even have read:

A A M E R L O V E S M A D E L I N E

Yasmine and Shahrukh brought it to me in a spirit of accusation. Safinaz sulked. Of course I denied I'd written it, told my parents it was a web of conspiracy woven by my sisters to trap me, shame me. I said they'd written it themselves. I might have cried with embarrassment, had I known how. I couldn't confess to writing Madeline's name or to my authorship of those words of love.

I'd only spoken to Madeline once. I think Fiona forced me to. For one day, for some reason, I found us sitting side by side, seating rules broken; perhaps two classes had been forced to study together because of the absence of a teacher. I can't remember what we said. I don't think there was a second time. Sometimes I wonder if I missed those sweaty cloakroom encounters with her, the meeting of hands and eyes and breath, the fear, the anger, the heat.

The White Lamb

My lamb had been taken away for shearing by Jiju, the erstwhile wrestler. He didn't show up once during the war, because of the curfew. But he did appear when it was over. He said his family had been hungry and the war had made things difficult; they'd killed and eaten the lamb. I remember my fists on his broad back, hammering it, the only time I ever hit anybody older or poorer, hammering until my mother, who'd sent the lamb away with him, pulled me off his back and made me apologise.

He used to tell stories, Jiju, about a princess whose husband thought she was dead because her maid betrayed her and took her place, and a green parrot who called to her across the water. When the princess asked the parrot, How much water, the parrot would respond, So much water, so she could cross the river when the tide was low to see and kiss her children while they slept. He had cauliflower ears, Jiju, and a cauliflower nose, because he'd been a fighter. Years later, I made him the hero of one of my stories, but the life I gave him was only half his.

Last year, a poem Faiz Ahmed Faiz once wrote in his lonely voice about cages and gardens and flowers and the breezes of spring became a runaway success as a song on the radio. Sometimes, half a mile from home, on our way to school, we'd see the poet in his garden.

The window of our classroom framed the sea. The waves lapped the sand ten steps away from the school wall. Further up there was a tongue of sand where you could stroll, play on a slide, or eat salt peanuts in newspaper cones on a Sunday. But by the time I left the convent, the local building authorities had started to reclaim land, and the sea was receding, giving way to tall structures of concrete and glass.

On my last day at school, the older girls came down and set up a disco in the assembly hall amid the statues of the Mater Dolorosa and the Pieta. Two of the tough girls, Roxane and my old pal Norwegian Helen, showed me how to french kiss under the piano. I heard Marianne Faithfull sing 'This little bird that somebody sent...' for the first time, and I learned the tune and most of the words in a sitting. We danced. Madeline must have been there: I can imagine her, surrounded by playmates, watching every move. I must have been performing for her. But she's invisible, I can't see her there.

I was going to Rome with my parents that night, my first trip westward. I had a party for my classmates and Safinaz's to say goodbye because the boys in my class were leaving school; the rest were going to the Brothers at St Pat's but I wanted to go to the American School or, failing that, to Karachi Grammar School where my cousins already were. All my classmates came to my farewell party. But Tina begged off at the last moment because her mother wouldn't let her go to parties attended or given by boys. And Madeline wasn't there. I don't remember whether she'd said she couldn't come or I hadn't got the message to her on time. Perhaps I hadn't invited her at all.

My farewell was a replay of the garden party my parents had given earlier that year. There were bags of sweets and comics for everyone from the lucky dip, and we played past sunset, till seven thirty, when cars came to take our playmates home. I left for the airport at midnight. It had been a year of parties.

La Befana

I should tell you about Rome: apricot juice and brioche at breakfast, hot chestnuts and La Befana the bearded Epiphany witch on Piazza Navona, the odious smell of parmesan, missing Safinaz, espressos sipped in pavement cafes on the Via Veneto, green suede shoes bought at Rafael's (is that how they spell it?), still missing Safinaz, movie diva Virna Lisi at a ball in a villa on the Appian Way naming me Bell'occhio (beautiful eyes) while I feel like a fop in my frilly white Roman shirt, the wind blowing the grey silk trousers of my grown-up suit against my thighs as importunate guides insist on speaking Spanish to my tall, dark-haired mother in her long red coat on the steps of St Peter's, missing Safinaz a little less, walking for miles in search of the English bookshop on Via Barberini – or was it Babbuino? – and the English cinema on Via...but I went back again to Rome eleven times at least in the next three decades and those memories are overlaid by later ones... all I see are the fountains of Tivoli, the streets of Pompei, the silver-tipped blue of the Bay of Naples in winter.

And yes, outside a restaurant somewhere near the Spanish

Steps, late on New Year's Night, an old fat Russian gipsy in the rain, black-and-white checked coat over her head like a nun's veil, playing the accordion, swaying, singing a merry drinking song...

Then we went to La Fontana di Trevi in the dark before morning. I got into the water, calf-deep, with Julie, a Swedish-American opera singer with whom I'd been singing Broadway duets that week. I cast my coins and wished I'd see Madeline again. I thought the fountain granted wishes.

Intermezzo

Many years later, when I was twenty-two, a friend of mine who'd fallen in love with Vanessa Redgrave in the role of Julia gave me the story by Lillian Hellman on which the film was based. That's how I read it, as a story, because I'd always felt good narrative should have the intensity of fiction, and the best stories carried the electric charge of lived experience. So, when people began to say that Hellman had never met Julia and her memoir was a figment of her diseased fantasies, I was bewildered. It was, after all, a fragment of her emotional life; I'd never expected it to be truthful in some photographic fashion. And as for films, they never pretend to be true to the texts they're taken from.

Stories are about finding the pattern, arranging elements

in a shape that makes sense. But now, faced with the chronology of my father's movements in the months that follow, I feel disinclined to explain, unable to deal in the documentary mode. Though every word I write here is as true as memory can make it, I'm merely chasing the flickering of light.

My friend Humma, who's spent time in Beijing, tells me the Chinese have an evocative name for images captured on film: Electric shadows.

ACT II

Majnoun

Daddy didn't come back to Karachi with us in January '66. He'd decided to stay on to see if he could make a new life for us: a few years in Rome, maybe, or in London. It was if he knew that horizons were shrinking at home, that all too soon Karachi wouldn't contain us, and we'd have to leave. Or else, by showing us how restless he was with our old life, the only one we'd ever had, he'd made us restless too, so that the desire to leave was, unwittingly, spreading its swallow wings in us, wings too fragile to catch or hold.

I battled with my mother over school. She didn't approve of my choices, because children at Karachi Grammar School spoke coarse English and swore, and American kids chewed gum. I didn't agree to her preference for an all-male establishment where emphasis was placed on physical training and good Urdu. Neither particularly appealed to me: I didn't like sports and the subtleties of the Arabic script bewildered me.

I spent those months at home reading: I'd developed a passion for history, but all you could find on the market in English were books about the Inquisition or the Armada, the Fall of Rome or the Sack of Jerusalem. In Urdu novels, you could read, in lush vivid language, about the Holy Prophet's time, or the Arabs in Granada and the Mughals in Lahore. I finally found heroes closer to home, with names like Aasim and Tariq, figures I could identify with. And then there was the legend of Kais, the one they called mad, Majnoun: in love with Laila, constantly writing messages to her on sand, hoping the desert wind would carry the grains of his love to her. Kais and Laila, cousins, shared my given name: they were the Children of 'Amer.

If I'd gone to the American School I'd have been with Madeline, who'd left Jesus and Mary at the same time as I had. I didn't seen her there any more when I went in the car to pick up my sisters.

(I did see Tina, though, as soon as I got back from Rome. I took her a bottle of scent – Ma Griffe, I think – which I'd bought for her on the plane. I presented it to her in front of a clapping crowd of ex-classmates. I was a little in love with her, but my faithful mind didn't have room for two loves, so I just thought of her as a friend.)

Borrowed Gold

Mehreen called Madeline again on 51112 – I don't know if I'd asked her to. And Madeline said she'd liked me very much but I hadn't paid her any attention, and later I seemed to like Tina. Then, at the exhibition, she saw Mehreen who was so beautiful and she thought Mehreen was my girl. Anywway, she was sort of seeing someone else. Some months later sweet Madeline left with her family for Islamabad and probably never shed a tear for her silent beau. Or maybe I melted into her violet dreams.

Karachi ceased to be the capital that year. Natives, who'd loved the coming and going of foreigners, would suddenly, on barbecue picnics beneath tamarind trees on cloudy days, throw up hands and voice a desire to be elsewhere, everything suddenly seemed to be happening somewhere else. And then they'd get on with parties and with living.

I never saw or heard from Madeline again.

(Tina I did speak to. For some reason her mother didn't allow her out, so we became telephone friends. She'd ring and tell the servants her name was Rani but I knew, of course, it was her and we'd be on the line for hours. At some point I walked the half-mile to her house by the ponds with my sister Shahrukh, to be told Tina was out. But her younger brother decided, for a fortnight or so, to be my best friend. He'd drive over to my gate in his Mercedes and take me out for a spin, or get dropped off at my house and spend the afternoon telling me very tall tales. I guess I wasn't very good company because I didn't play cricket or talk much and spent my time reading weighty books. One day we were playing about by some thorny bushes on the footpath that led down the hill our house was on when something he did provoked me to run off and he followed and twisted my arm behind my back until I saw stars and fell. I wasn't used to being touched by boys. I'd never really liked boys very much, apart from two or three at school. The friendship with Tina's brother was over and though I didn't hold Tina's brother's ways against her I don't remember speaking to Tina again after that. She might have gone away, to a boarding school in Murree.)

In the seventh century after our prophet, the poet Sa'di sang:

O camel driver, drive slowly, for my soul's rest is leaving,
and with her the heart I thought was mine is leaving

But I'd learned, after Snowy and Madeline, not to want what I couldn't have or what threatened to disappear. In spite of the letters erased from the slate, in spite of my name, I was neither father nor son of that Kais bin 'Amer who pines in the sands for Laila and spends his hours kissing the letters of her name. Love feeds on the anticipation of what you know will come back, it grows and thrives. But there are summer days that betray you with their borrowed gold. Love fades when you know you're longing for nothing. Your hands grasp air. Love chokes on absence.

Pause

In our garden, between the almond tree and the hibiscus, there's a fountain of yellow-white stone. The white lamb loved to drink there. Sometimes I think I hear the sound of her bleating or her collar's blue bells behind me in the garden.But Madeline, when I look in the water for her reflection, just isn't there. In her place there's a shadow of shame and guilt.

Love goes, I learn: hurt remains.

So where, you will ask, has my story gone? Faded away with Madeline, with Tina, colours dimmed almost to sepia?

Sit still. I have other loves to speak of. It's already April, where my tale began last year. Only five pages of the calendar left to turn.

Waiting. Patiently.

The light flickers.
   I wait for my father to come back.
   I turn eleven, quietly, without a party.

Mother Tongue

May. There's a downpour. We come out of a cinema that's showing *The Unsinkable Molly Brown*. Outside, among the puddles, our car stands driverless. We have to wait for the chauffeur to come back with the key. When he does, my mother sacks him on the spot and drives the six miles home in the thunderstorm through the swelling flood.

   Mother has been looking after Daddy's fishing trawler business while he's away. She's incongruous there; I always wonder how she keeps her fine cottons from soaking up smells of fish. For a while, I go with her to the harbour at West Wharf, where boats come in with nets full of lobsters and prawns, to look over accounts and oversee affairs, as I'd loved to do with my father when he was here; I don't mind the fish smell.

   But then our car breaks down and I sell it as scrap, and Mother decides to send Rahmatullah, a servant she trusts, to work on the boats. He has other ideas. No money comes in for weeks at a time. By the time he's made off with most of the profits it's too late to catch up with him.

And Daddy's had a heart attack in Rome; then another one in London. (He'd probably left Rome because it must have been terrifying to stay in a hospital and try to communicate in a language he barely knew.) So plans for him to come and wind up matters in Karachi, to take us to a new place, are on hold till he's well enough to conclude arrangements and deals.

We don't dare to think what might happen if his heart and his health get worse.

The night musicians still pass our lane after sundown, though their songs are more distant now. I can tell some of their stories: of Mahiwal and Rano and Punhal Baloch, heroes damned to misery. I can sing all their songs, but I don't know the words.

For three or four months I've been walking an enchanted tightrope between yesterday and tomorrow, waiting for Daddy to send a message that will be *the* message. Or I read for hours on the leafy branches of the almond tree while Yasmine works, unpaid, as editorial assistant for my aunt's fashion magazine, and Shah and Safinaz still go to school in a neighbour's car. I enter the pages of a glorious past, written, in the cursive loops of a script that always eludes me, into the intimate pleasures of my mother tongue.

June. Sandstorms rise. White grains in waves, blowing on winds hot as iron, harsh as glass. Three days like hell: we draw the drapes and lie beneath the fan. Unbearable. Imam Hussein and the Martyrs were deprived of water on days parched and burnt like these.

Then the locust swarms. Thick and black on the wind, you can't step out, the mass is too dense. But the gardener is there, screaming: My fruit, my flowers, all gone, everything, in two hours, just two hours, they strip each single tree of foliage. Only thorns survive. And Mother says: Plants always grow again.

There's a story she once told us, about the boy called Shravan who carried his parents on his back from place to place in search of a cure for their ailment, but when he reached the desert, barren land with its spiky cactus and the angry white sun above, he put them down on the thirsty sand. No water here to drink, he said, only mirages. I can't carry you any more. Sometimes, in summer, our city looks like her story's barren land.

In summer, when there's drought, we turn off the fountain. Leaves from the almond tree fall into its emptiness.

Mother has come home with a headache today. It worsens as the day wears on. Then she's delirious. Her four children, alone, my oldest sister seventeen and our youngest ten, phone every doctor whose number we can lay hands on. No one agrees to come. *It's the weekend. We're too busy. I'm a gynaecologist. I don't do home visits.*

Finally a second cousin sends a novice relative who takes one look at Mother and diagnoses meningitis. She's been ill three days, maybe longer, hours of light and darkness have merged. The ambulance arrives to take her away in just under an hour. Six hours more without a lumber puncture and you'd have lost her, the doctor says. You'd better fumigate the rooms after she's left.

...When will he come back, the redeemer, the dreamer, with eyes that carry the sea in their shallows, little paper boats of passage on his palms...

That summer, while Mother lies in her hospital bed, the rains come down on us so heavy that the streets flood and for unending days no one will risk driving us over to see her.

... Hands folded in prayer or clutching each other's, words or wishes soundless on tips of tongues, we lie awake these restless nights, begging the God we never see, save us from rain, Lord of Mercy, bring our missing ones home...

By the time Daddy comes home two months later to relieve us, delayed three times by the hazards of transnational flights, I've forgotten Jesus and Mary and all the friends I had there, who've gone their way with the leaves of my cabbage. And though I hardly know this now, and I still think my father's light makes my lost leaves grow back, soon I'll realise that my mother has taken his place as the one for whom I keep the heart of the cabbage I am.

Mother's in hospital when Daddy returns. But she comes home a few weeks after. She has to lie down much of the time. She's so sensitive to sudden noise that we make a bed for her in what had been the dining room. She'll sit up by a picture window overlooking a bed of sunflowers she planted.

Beside the sunflower grows its papery twin, a flower with a name no one knows.

Daddy sits by Mother's bed with his head bowed over folded hands. He seems to be praying. Violet shadows spread around his eyes.

Leavetaking

In September, barely a year after the war, when Pakistan's fraught relationship with India is at its lowest ebb in the nineteen years since independence, we're invited to my cousin's wedding in Bombay. When we decide to go, without our parents who'll follow four weeks later, we have no way of knowing we're leaving behind the house for ever.

Mehreen doesn't know how to say goodbye. She taps my cheeks with her fingertips; little slaps in lieu of a caress.

We will come back to Karachi – in April – but by then our

landlady has died. In our absence, her daughter and her grandson have reclaimed the house and put our stuff in storage with our aunt next door. We've come back only to leave.

Lena the dachschund, boarding with friends, has betrayed my sisters: she's become so fat she waddles, and she answers now to the name of Lottie. We stay with our aunt till December that year. We never again will have a home of our own in Karachi.

There are days that betray you with their borrowed gold. Childhood pleasures are no armour for future adversity. I won't see Karachi again for twenty-nine years, and when I do go back my name will have a different spelling.

Electric Shadows

Only five years after leaving, in another country on another continent, I decided, as dreamers often do, that I should be someone, make a mark on life: fill a space, even a small one, with songs, soothe the scars on people's souls with words, or write and make a difference in the world. When I began to write my tales, that's what I planned to do, make a difference, I thought stories could right wrongs, dilute injustices, but though it took five years I knew mine never really would, I wasn't here to make a difference, only to be insignificant, because all I did was work and dream and wait for life to happen to me. And sometimes I'd think of all those wordless songs I'd sung, of Madeline and my sins of omission, how I'd started then the pattern of stillness that wasn't yet erased, of stepping back and letting someone else speak for me, of writing secret words of love to which I never would admit. I hadn't even chosen my first love for myself. And my stories, too, are happenstance; electric shadows of chance encounters and changing love. But then sometimes I think of what has come to me so easily, much more than I have ever missed, or things I often didn't want at all; echoes of memories spill their light into my nights, I wish day had more hours and night more places of solace, and I think that for a life so still mine's really been quite full. And what I've longed for, well, longing bears within it the message and the promise of its own fulfilment. The image of a golden head bent over a desk dissolves into the picture of a peach stolen from a farmyard in summer. Fresh lake water trickles down my shoulder blade beneath a white sky. The smell of jasmine wafts in through my bedroom window. The sunflower talks to its papery twin. One hand trembles with the weight of words that make a captive of love.

What Do You Call Those Birds?

The waters of the ocean are pure, my
*   friend*
Remember love will last but two days:
And its pain a lifetime endure

(from a Punjabi wedding song)

1

That summer they met, before the storm that brought down branches and set the year apart for Londoners, Iman and Sameer, birds of passage both, were the best of friends. Sameer was thirty-one, beginning to sell stories, and working as an itinerant reviewer of books and films while he researched a thankless thesis contrasting the phenomenological approaches of Sartre and Klein. Iman, four years younger, was the elegant books editor of a politically-orientated current affairs magazine; she commissioned pieces by Sameer on a fairly regular basis, but she'd also decided that her real task was to launch him as a burgeoning talent in a world she knew was fickle.

Apart from a shared love for exotic food and bizarre films, Iman and Sameer also had Karachi in common. In an odd way, though. He had left the city of his birth as a teenager in the year that Iman, still a child, had been relocated there by her family who were evading the ire of Idi Amin. But soon she'd moved back, to boarding schools in East Africa. Though Sameer always thought of her – with her tall, pale Kashmiri prettiness, her gentle Urdu and her almost traditionally formal manners – as a Pakistani, Iman was a child of the new Africa; her mental landscapes, which she would sometimes recreate in oil on paper, were in ochres, browns and greens he found hard to recognise. Iman had spent her life between three worlds and three languages, one world more than Sameer was used to. Karachi, which was gradually fading away from him, was a place she sometimes visited for fun, while Africa to her was a kind of refuge, the place she returned to when she had wounds to heal.

And Sameer soon found out that reticent Iman had wounds, deep and many, that needed to heal. Behind the laughter and the evasions was a fragile, even shattered, sense of her place in the world. Rainy days followed the storm. They were neighbours in Maida Vale; after a film or a Thai dinner they'd often go to one of their flats and settle over a pot of green tea to talk half the night away. Or they'd persuade a friendly local pizzeria owner to keep open till late for coffee and cakes. They became close: Sameer told her he'd recently become involved with a flighty married woman of whose vodka-inspired antics Iman, when she'd seen them together in a cafe, hadn't approved. Iman confessed that she was on the verge of divorce, from a man who wouldn't let her go but couldn't keep her happy; she'd married Yasir when they were still only students, but passion had worn out when seven years of his drinking and profligate spending had dulled her response, and rumours of his polymorphously perverse orgies on Mediterranean cruises had reached her.

2

They'd been friends just over a year, their closeness only hindered by the demands on their time of others who claimed even greater closeness. Then Iman – after a bad experience setting up a fashion magazine on a millionairess acquaintance's narcissistic whim – suddenly decided to leave London, her nearly-former husband and her brightening career. She decided, too, to give up the book world and go for business economics. She found a job that would send her to Hong Kong. She wrote Sameer loving messages on post cards and once dropped in for a fleeting visit. But for the better part of eighteen months, in which he missed her sorely, their lives diverged.

And by the time she came back, Sameer's life had changed. His career had taken off – like a raft rather than a plane, but all the same it was moving.

He had three stories anthologised that summer. On Iman's advice he'd abandoned post-graduate research, but now had a two-year contract teaching in the modern languages department of a university. On the other hand, his relationship with his now-divorced woman friend was in perilous depths. Mona was always jealous, imagining non-existent rivals, particularly after he'd been too friendly for a season with a young – and unmarried – visiting scholar and he'd even, fleetingly, contemplated marriage. That Ayla had soon told him she was on the rebound from someone else was hardly, Mona thought, of any consequence: fantasy betrayals were as bad as the real thing. Of course Sameer, too, had been on the rebound from a relationship that was moving very fast in no direction.

3

'Sameer?'

He heard Iman's voice on the phone on a sunny morning in April, after six months of silence. He was recovering from one of Mona's worst onslaughts on his job, his stories, his friendships and his moral integrity.

'Iman, where the hell have you been?'

'Karachi! Didn't you ever get the card with my address?'

'What, where, when, why...?'

'Don't ask any questions. Just meet me in that new cafe by the canal.'

'But...'

'I flew in last night. With Yasir.'

'Yasir?'

'Yes, Yasir! He *is* my husband, you know? We're back together again. Don't ask any more questions. Just get yourself over to La Ville for a cappuccino.'

Iman, in those days, was always, notoriously, late. Sameer stood, waiting about fifteen or twenty minutes, for her blue car to drive down Blomfield Road. The café was closed. It was a sunny Monday.

Then she was there.

'Yes', she said as they sat over sandwiches and Perriers in a stained-glass and stucco pub they found a minute's walk away,

'I went back to Yasir. You know we never really did divorce. He followed me to Karachi...'

'What's with the Karachi story? You were happy as a lark in Hong Kong last time we talked...'

'Hong Kong gets lonely for a single person especially if you aren't part of an expat set. I didn't really get on well with the Cantonese. Talk about closed circles. I'd go off to Beijing because I love the people there but the language problem's even worse. I couldn't cope with the food, too much offal: I picked up a bug and was sick all the time. I went back to Hong Kong and it was freezing. The sea looked like glass, as if at any moment it might break. Then Desmond – my editor, you'll remember him – rang me and said there was an office opening in Karachi. I could go there on a longish assignment. I leapt at the chance. Our house there in Clifton was lying empty. It's beautiful, just by the sea, one of those sandy spots where you can still see the sea in fact, and it never gets too hot because of the sea breezes.

'Karachi's fun after London, your phone always ringing, someone inviting you out every day. We were euphoric about having a woman ruling after ten years of seeing that ogre in power. The new regime had things under control, even if you could feel the tension, like a time bomb, under the surface, with policemen on the streets, and people saying it wasn't really safe to drive around alone as I did. Half the time I was too tired to go out anyway, writing reports and articles and virtually running the office, but it's nice to know there's something to do whenever you want to. And the weather...after so many years of rain I'd started hearing dripping water in my sleep. I almost enjoyed the humidity and the heat. I have lots of friends there from my Grammar School days – many of them are married now, some divorced. They'd drag me out to hotels for dinner or to their homes. I never knew there were so many picnic spots a few miles away from the city. Have you been inland to see those lakes and hidden creeks? The pollution in Karachi's bad, but out there it's as clean as unspoilt parts of Africa.

'Everyone was always trying to pair me off, get me married. Men call you all the time. And you know me, I'm spontaneous enough, I love having men as friends, but I'm cautious too. Some of those men are ready for a fling with their best friend's wife or their wife's best friend ...they call you when their wives are off shopping in Singapore or Manhattan, and you have to learn to be busy all the time. The only problem is, when you brush them off, they look out for you in public places or in the passenger seat of a car with any man, eligible or not, and the next minute you're either about to be married, or stealing your best friend's husband. But not everyone's like that. Take Kashif...'

'How in hell do you expect me to know who Kashif is without yet another of your long asides, Iman? You were going to tell me about Yasir. How did he track you down? I was convinced that half the reason you were running away from London was to get him off your back. Don't you remember all those midnight calls after which you'd ring me at two in the morning? And the time he followed us from Knightsbridge and we found him parked outside your garage half asleep...'

'God, you've got a great memory for embarrassing moments. But you know it wasn't always like that. He can be good company sometimes, generous, and he can make me laugh. You know what the real reason is? I married him just after my twenty-first birthday. At twenty-three I had my first abortion when he said we couldn't afford a baby because he was thinking of moving us to Harvard so he could do his MBA. And he'd promised to get me back into my post-grad work too. Anyway, after that time and the miscarriage I had later I've always thought, if I have a baby, it has to be his. That's the reason. Now's the time. I'm thirty.

'When he started ringing me up in Karachi – don't even ask how he found my number, a friend told me he'd started getting so drunk and weeping so desperately that he couldn't bear not to give it to him – when he started ringing me up every night, would you believe...I felt sorry for him? And he was so far away...I could just sense his anguish, and the old tenderness came back, you know how lovely his voice can be when he's like that.'

It had taken Yasir, she told Sameer, nine months to break down the door of her reserve. One day she found flowers at her door, then again, and on the third day they were attached to a lyric in his handwriting and a compact disc of 'I Will Always Love You' – the Dolly Parton version she loved.

'He was in Karachi,' Iman said. 'He'd found an excuse, and come after me, all the way. I saw him for lunch, then a week or so later for dinner. He started off on the old stuff again, and I said I didn't want to go back, only forward. He said he'd give me time, as much time as I wanted, to make up my mind. Then he went off to see his family in Pindi and Faisalabad. When he came back he asked me for a fresh start, to live with him again. It was the first night of a new decade. Like the first time he'd asked me to spend my life with him. And I said yes.'

4

But Iman and Yasir stayed together only till the end of the next year. She didn't get pregnant; he found himself in trouble over a phony deal with a Greek and a credit card scam. When Iman told him to stay where he was (in Nicosia, if Sameer remembers rightly) and not bother coming back because she'd changed the locks, Yasir cleared out all the money from their deposit account, left her with their double mortgage, and went back to Mummy in Pakistan. As usual, Iman escaped to the healing powers of her African landscape. But Africa was also becoming a place of passage for her restless wings: too long in Uganda, and the lures of North or South would entice her again, and it would be London or Karachi for her, with shorter spells in Lombok or Istanbul, Dusseldorf or Prague. And she'd move just as restlessly from writing to painting on canvas or textiles or practising her calligraphy. Then she came back to London with a plan. She was finally going to get that post-graduate degree, from Birkbeck this time, so she could take two years over it and work once again as a journalist and freelance editor to earn her way.

That year – it must have been '92 – Sameer was working overtime to finish his first book of fiction, which was scheduled for the following year. Since several stories of his were coming out in print here and there he'd sometimes be called upon to appear at bookshops, theatres and galleries, to read or sign books, or simply join in celebrations.

Things had come full circle now. Five years or six years ago, Iman would call him at the last minute from her office: 'The Parrot Club *now*. Maya Angelou's launching a book. There's someone I'm seeing there – a brilliant black editor you MUST meet. She's involved with a new publishing company. Okay. Come late if you want to. Dinner later at Mr Chow's.'

Sameer would leave his typewriter, shower, put on something studiedly casual, and find his way to Lower Sloane Street and her in the rush hour. Iman not only gave him his first ever cheque for a review; she actually showed him the way round the life of a London writer. Book launches, review copies, agents, publicity schedules were words in a foreign vocabulary Sameer had acquired from her.

Now he was the one who dragged Iman from his own signings to a friend's launch and on to dinner with another gang of writers and actors and hacks. She was used to them; she smiled and joked; she occasionally, laconically announced to them she was a first-rate talent spotter because she'd spotted Sameer and been there for him from the start. If he was the one to mention how she'd discovered him she'd say: 'When they told us at school that Speke discovered the source of the Nile I'd say nonsense, the source of the Nile was already there, how can some colonial have discovered it? Of course I didn't discover Sameer. Just like the source of the Nile, he was already there.'

But she never once tried to re-establish literary connections or fish for a commission, preferring to write quiet reports for specialist journals, on slavery, human rights and international trade; and, always, Africa.

More often than not, now, they'd leave parties early, to dine in one of their old South East Asian haunts in Maida Vale, or look for a new place for Laksa and Indonesian noodles. Sometimes, after a gruelling session at Birkbeck, she'd come and pick him up from wherever he was, and they'd go somewhere to walk by water and look at swans: Windsor,

Marlowe, or just Hyde Park. (Over the years, Iman and Sameer, they've seen swans at every hour of the evening, even in rain and chilly autumn. This summer they've befriended a black swan they saw once preening its wings with its vermilion beak as the sun set in the river.)

But their hearts were heavier than they'd been six years ago. Then she'd hidden her hurt behind the smoke screen of literary chat, while he'd still been excited enough by the call of a vocation to live for tomorrow. If they fell short of cash they'd walk around in Chinatown for hours, then end up pooling their remaining money to give five pounds to a homeless black man they'd adopted who camped on the junction of Charing Cross Road and Oxford Street and who swore murderously at them. Now Iman was a diligent student again, and Sameer had found that the grooming he was getting for his own five minutes of fame was like any other job — only, at times, more exhausting. Mona had finally fled London for Karachi when he started writing too frenetically and asked, as she left, for a permanent rain check on their relationship. So he, too, had been on his own for more than a year. (But all that, and the nervous breakdown the horrors of the Gulf War nearly gave him, are part of another story, which Sameer has yet to tell and probably never will.)

One evening Iman waited for Sameer outside an old brownstone in Aldwych for twenty minutes. A ginger-whiskered publisher had been trying to push his newest two-minute Indian superstar's ethnic epic at him and he thought Iman would be furious he'd kept her waiting. She wasn't. She didn't often smoke, but while she waited she'd lit up a silver-tipped low tar. He noticed, in the last rays of the evening sun, that she'd cut and highlighted her brown hair. She grinned and said:

'Tandoori tonight. There's someone I'm dying for you to to meet.'

She parked her car just off Euston Square. The restaurant they went to was modest outside, and the minimalist interior was bare, white and just bright enough. Abida Parveen sang softly in the background – 'tera ishq nachaya, thayya thayya'. Sameer didn't ask Iman who they were going to meet, he was used to being joined at supper by one or another of her erstwhile Canterbury colleagues, with or without spouses in tow. Iman walked up to ask the head waiter something, then handed him a folded note. He nodded the indeterminate nod that implies 'maybe', then Sameer saw the sharper sideways tilt that indicates a definite negation.

Next, a robust, long-haired man who'd had one or two lurched up from his corner table with a pint glass in his hand and gave Iman that ghastly clap on the shoulder blade they called the Punjabi salute. Sameer saw a flicker of anguish on her forehead for a second and then, perfectly composed, she brought him over to their table. She had a tenderness for waifs, strays and stragglers, and Sameer was terrified she'd ask her friend to join them at their tiny table. He couldn't think why she'd wanted them to meet.

'Sameer, meet Niaz. Niaz Hassan, you know, the director? He's not staying, such a pity, he says he just made other plans on his mobile. He's been waiting for Kashif, too. Niaz, this is my friend Sameer, the budding literary genius, you know. You should get him to write a script for you.'

5

'What do you call those birds, Sameer?'

Iman looked up at the purple sky. Greyish birds with black-tipped wings were dipping down and skimming the Serpentine, probably to fish up scraps of bread or other flotsam from the water's turbid surface.

'Gulls, I suppose. Can't be seagulls, though, so far away from the sea.'

'And those ones at the seaside in Karachi?'

'I don't call them anything, Iman, I don't remember birds at the seaside in Karachi. Curlews? Cormorants?'

'The ones you see at night. They're tiny white birds, really little...'

'Tiny white birds you see at night? I don't know, I left Karachi before I ever had a chance to see birds on the beach at night, and anyway you know I'm not an ornithologist. Now tell me about those friends of yours at the restaurant.'

'Niaz directs films for TV, smart soaps with a moral. Kashif's a friend of both of ours. He left a message on my machine for me to meet him there, then he didn't show up. Have you ever thought of writing a teleserial, or a play, Sameer? I bet you could do it and then I'll give it to Niaz.'

'Oh, so it was Niaz you wanted me to meet. To peddle my wares to him.' Sameer had tried for a crusty tone, but he was laughing. Iman slipped her cool hand into his.

'No, silly, I didn't even know he was going to be there. But listen. Seriously. Why don't you write for him?'

'I love Karachi TV soaps. I'd die to write one. But they want family dramas, feuds, marriages, breakups – I couldn't write such stories.'

'I've got great ideas. I'll tell you one.'

'Over coffee? There's a chill breeze blowing.'

6

'I met Kashif when I'd just gone back to Karachi in '89. I was quite lonely, and as I said men around could be predatory, particularly if they knew I was divorced. I'd met him even before I got engaged to Yasir, but I never got to know him. This time I ran into him at a coffee shop with friends, and though he didn't say much to me I liked him immediately. You remember that story you wrote, about a man with very blue eyes? That's what I immediately thought of when I saw Kashif, that he looked like one of these blue-eyed devils you write about. But he wasn't a devil at all. He's from a respectable, middle class family, Kashmiri like mine, but soon someone told me he was in trouble over a girl, or rather that he'd got involved with a girl his parents didn't approve of. Then, because I drove around all over Karachi on my own, I'd keep bumping into him. When he asked me to have a croissant and coffee with him at the Pearl Continental, I didn't see how there could be any harm.

'That's when he told me about Sania. He'd started seeing her when he was eighteen – their parents were friends, even distantly related – and by the time they were in their twenties they were engaged. But recently things had gone terribly wrong. Their fathers had fought, then their mothers; it may have been over dowry, or a promise he believed his father may have made to Sania's, to help him out with his flagging garment business. Sania and he had begun to grow apart, but they'd decided to give it time, until, suddenly, Sania's father collapsed into his dinner plate one night because a paper had printed the news that he was bankrupt, and five days later his heart stopped beating. Sania blamed Kashif's family for his death and now she was working at a travel agency to support her mother, a younger brother and a sister. He'd offered to help, financially, but she'd accused him of trying to offload his responsibilities and then cried, saying he wanted to abandon her.

'Then I remembered: I'd met Sania. Once. She was attractive, in a florid Punjabi manner. What came back to me vividly, though, wasn't the way she looked: it was the weird story she'd been telling. She said she'd gone to see a psychic because she was suffering from a chronic stomach ailment which made her bleed and bleed and she'd been told that an old, jealous woman had put the evil eye on her. The psychic gave Sania some coloured powder which he told her to bake in a little bun with some white flour and place that on the highest wall for the birds to eat, every day at sunrise, for a week. Sania said she baked the buns with the powder every day and placed them on the wall but they just lay drying there in the harsh sunlight, the birds wouldn't touch them and she kept getting sicker and sicker. She was convinced that her future mother-in-law had cast the evil eye on her, so that she'd die of the blood she was losing, and Kashif would be free to marry another, richer girl. She said what Kashif's family had against hers was that they hadn't been able to give him the money to go to Harvard for further education. On the last day of that week Sania baked the last batch of buns with all the powder she had left. Soon she saw, from the window, a swarm of crows descending. Later in the day she went out to see: there were many dead crows, some on the wall, some on the dusty ground below. She screamed and ran to get the sweeper to take them away to the garbage dump. The next day she simply stopped bleeding.'

'Kashif and I became friends,' Iman said in the Soho coffee bar they'd found open, as she lit up a cigarette she'd taken from Sameer's pack. 'At first we'd meet during the day, for coffee or a snack, or just go shopping for curios together, me for the Clifton house, he for his restaurants in London. Most often, we'd talk on the phone: he'd usually call at night. It became a habit. I'd come home in time for his call. I couldn't sleep if I missed it. That's when Yasir had started calling too; once Kashif called and I said Oh, Yasir, because I'd just told Yasir to get off the line; so I was forced to pour it all out to him, about Yasir, the marriage, the separation, the divorce I hadn't taken, the decision, to leave him or go back, I still had to make.

'That evening Kashif suggested we have dinner and then go for a drive to the sea. We talked about our respective relationships, his fraying so badly there seemed no purpose in trying to mend it, mine on ice. Yasir had gone off just then, to give me some time; he was with his family in Pindi.

'We'd just finished eating our fresh prawns with crispy noodles. Kashif said: Have you ever seen the seabirds? Which ones? I asked. He called them by some local name that started with a syllable like cha or sha. (Maybe, Sameer, you know the word.) Come on, I'll take you to see them, he said.

'It was one of those winter nights, moonless, but the light seemed to come from the water and a sprinkling of stars in that very, very dark Karachi sky. We walked down the cliff

I wish to be kept informed of your new publications and events

Subjects in which I have a special interest

☐ Art & Architecture ☐ History ☐ Politics ☐ Anthropology

☐ Women's Studies ☐ Fiction ☐ Poetry ☐ Languages

Other interests: ....

Name ....

Address ....

....

....

Postcode .... Country ....

E-mail ....

Your requests can also be sent by e-mail to: saqibooks@dial.pipex.com

not far away from where I lived – it was still pretty quiet and empty three years ago – and found a place beneath a rock. We were slightly cold, but he'd brought a Sindhi shawl from the car. The sand was shining. He told me to close my eyes and only open them when he'd counted to ten. I shut them. He counted. Then he said, look! And I opened my eyes. I'd never seen anything like it. I've never seen anything comparable since. Dozens of little birds, coming down to drink, playing on the crest of the tide. Some were riding the waves like horses. Little greyish white birds. Not beautiful, perhaps, but prettier than sparrows, and quite luminous in the sealight. The whispering water was full of their shadows. I don't know, Sameer, I tell you. Sometimes I think it was a trick of the light, something that happens when moonbeams refract from rock to water, mirage or hallucination. But that night it took my breath away. When I turned, I noticed Kashif, who'd taken my hand in his for the first time, was crying, actually crying.

'On the way back he told me he loved me, that he'd loved me from the start. I didn't respond. Then he kissed my eyes. I knew he'd tried really hard with Sania, like I'd tried for at least the last three years with Yasir, but Sania was giving him a bad, bad time, and as for me, I didn't know whether it was regret, pity or self-vindication that compelled me to give Yasir a moment more than the time of day. You know what it's like. You can put everything into a relationship but when there's only ugliness coming from the other person, you start to retreat, to wither, at least if you're someone like me.

'Don't, Kashif said as I got down from his jeep, don't go back to Yasir. Whatever you do.

'He was asking me to wait. I knew I'd be all right with him. After all these years, he'd made me feel something again, something fragile, but there. I didn't answer. I didn't make plans. That's where we left it. I knew he'd call me the next day. He didn't. I tried his mobile number. No answer. I didn't hear from him for three days.

'On the fourth day,' Iman said, in her car on the way back to Maida Vale, 'he showed up at my door. It was Christmas, '89. I'd made plans for that evening with a couple of friends visiting from Bangkok. He wouldn't come inside. He looked – devastated. He said, we have to talk, Iman. I can't remember what I said to him about that evening's plans, or whether I asked him where he'd been all these days, but I knew I had to go with him, wherever he took me, however far away.

'He drove in silence for more than two hours. I don't even know if he drove past the airport into Sindh or by the sea to Baluchistan. I know the landscape changed colour, became redder and rockier, and I thought for a moment I was back in East Africa.

'He stopped the jeep at an unforgettable place: rugged, austere, but beautiful. It made me think of those lines from the Surah of the Benificent: How many of His wonders will you deny? On the banks of a deep, deep creek in which silver water flowed there were tufts of tall grass and yellow flowers that looked like dahlias nestling in the sparse green. Dragonflies darted here and there. One of those scenes that make you realise how small you are in the scheme of things.

'We got out and walked. I'm not going to try to remember his words. Nor the reasons he gave. He had to marry Sania. Just had to. His parents, furious, were saying they'd disown him. His brothers were boycotting the wedding. He didn't know what to do. But he couldn't let Sania down. He was marrying her on the second day of the New Year.

'Don't marry her, I said, and I didn't register his response, till I understood what he was saying.

'I need a sister to stand by me, Kashif said. Someone to lead the wedding procession, welcome the bride, dance and sing. Will you play my sister on the day of my wedding?

'I can't remember what I said, but I knew I'd do it for him, even if my feet hurt while I danced. I looked at a kite or an eagle wheeling overhead: I hoped Kashif's small white birds didn't come here to get eaten, and I thought, I'm going to say yes to Yasir when he comes back on New Year's Eve, and next year, perhaps, I'll have a baby.'

7

Sameer's first book came out the following year. Iman had

flown over from Kampala to be with him. Not exactly: she'd been in London a while, had radical surgery just before, but she staggered bravely out of bed, put on makeup and some traditional Kashmiri embroidery, and drove him to his party.

For the rest of the decade, after taking her degree, she flew restlessly between Kampala, London and Karachi, freelancing, always between homes. But she didn't see Kashif again, though they spoke on the telephone from time to time. Yasir had settled down in Pindi and had two children. Strange, Iman said to Sameer one day, how some men learn to settle and love only after battering one woman almost to death. I hope he's happy wherever he is as long as he's out of my life.

Sameer wrote another book. He was finishing it while Iman fell in love again. She said she'd never yet known what passion was until she met the younger divorced man she called Dr K. Then she found out he was still married, and he later told her that his wife was pregnant. Their affair went on for nearly three years, till the end of the decade, even after she'd found him out. Sameer didn't approve. It's your business, he said; it's your life, he still says.

As the nineties breathed their last, Sameer flew off to see his sister in Bangladesh, having missed the topography of his stories for two years. Iman, who'd got her younger brother married the year before to a suitable woman, a blend of brilliance with beauty, wanted to spend the dawn of the millenium with them in Africa.

Sameer wasn't able to see Iman till after his birthday in April. She was upset. She thought he'd changed. He hasn't. Iman means more to him than ever.

Now they meet often. Their contentious conversations are in English; for affection they move to Urdu. But then, again, their mother tongue does well for blessings and moral advice. (A week ago, at one of their old coffee hangouts in Little Venice, Iman told Sameer she'd seen her phantom love again. Sameer shook his head, tut-tutting. Your life, he said, not my place to disapprove. No, Iman replied, don't worry about us. We met and talked. It's gentler now, like finding a pressed flower you left once between the pages of a book. The fragrance has gone, and you've forgotten its perfume. But you remember the touch of it.)

8

At 1 am on the 21st of May 2000 Sameer rang Iman to tell her he was finally in the middle of writing her story.

'Not a soap opera,' he said, 'but I've made you the heroine of a tale. And I hope you don't expect me to have all the facts right.'

She said: 'A story, don't you think, is as real as the reader makes it?'

But there were things Sameer still wanted to know. He asked if she ever found out what the little white birds were called that she'd seen at the seaside in Karachi, and what the name of the lake was that she walked by near her house in Kampala.

'Lake Victoria,' Iman said. 'Funny you should ask. I walked there to see the last sunset of the century and I thought of birds, and of the places I'd been to with Kashif, the rocks of the beach at night and the reddish-ochre of the creek. At Lake Victoria there are gulls and you can sometimes see flamingos. And crested cranes. I saw a crested crane that night I was there. Would you believe it was dancing? One foot forward, one foot back, head high then dipping, by the shores of the lake. The sun was about to go down and the lake was the colour of jade. And my mind travelled back ten years to Kashif's wedding night. How I danced. There she was, in front of me, Sania in her transparent yellow wedding veil, she muttered something to her bridegroom when she saw me as I came up like a sister would do, to take some ransom money from his pocket, and she said, what's this woman doing here? But I didn't care. I joined the dancing girls on the floor. Some sang and others beat the wedding drums. My hands in the air, my feet hit the ground. I thought of seas and lakes, and birds on their shores, and how next year I might have a baby, and I danced.'

The City of Longing

*One Wednesday when the blooming sun
    suffused with blue the sky's black dome,
The King, victorious as the sun, bright sky-
    like robes of turquoise donned,
Went to the turquoise dome for sport, the tale
    was long, the day was short.*

Nizami of Ganja, *Haft Paikar* (1197).
(Translated from the Persian by Julie Scott
Meisami)

You have come now to the city of men who wear black: you
will want to know why our garb is so sombre. This is the city
where night never falls. But there is often a scarcity of light,

when lowering clouds loom above us for days and no rain comes. A city of endless gloomy day. But we have time. Sit down here, on the wall. Smoke a pipe with us, and drink a glass of tea. A desert wind blows around us. Soon it will touch your cheek with the ice of Siberia. But we have time. The coals in the brazier are glowing. Sit down and we will tell you our tale. You may decide to follow the path we took. Or you may take our words as warning: ours is not the path of the faint-hearted.

So listen: When you leave the city's northern gate, you will come to a rocky hill, hard to climb. Take off your shoes at the foot of this hill. Ascend. Reach its peak.

There you will find a pavilion of stone, formed like a basket. It rests on one rock, suspended from four woven chains. Observe these chains with care: they, too, are carved of stone. Look up, towards the sky. If your eyesight is good you will see, far, far up amid the clouds, the hovering wings of a great bronze eagle.

Your feet will be sore. Bloody, perhaps. You may want to turn back but you'll need to rest. Because there is no other place, you will enter, by climbing over its woven wall, the pavilion, which is large enough for one man only. You will feel a sudden tremor, and the basket, straw-light now, will rise in the air. Buffeted by wind and rain, you will rise till the vessel that carries you comes to rest on a dark cloud. You will feel it shatter around you, shards falling about you in showers.

Then the great bronze eagle, free now from its burden, will swoop down on you to take you in its beak. You will feel the flames of its eyes on your face, you will smell its carrion breath. You might faint.

Have you, our fine young friend, a head for heights?

Sleep if you can. The journey is long, the journey is short.

You will wake to find yourself, naked and sweating in your shreds, on a narrow islet swimming on a wide silver river. No bird, no basket here. You will want to look for leaves to cover your shame, but isn't it better to rinse your sore body in the warm currents of water instead, wash off the weariness of your journey through the clouds?

Enter the river. Close your eyes.

You will open them to see around you a bevy of tender women, their hair and eyes of every colour, their hands soft like the satins of China. They will rub your limbs with water fragrant as the oils of Arabia. The tiny lashes of their fingers will play on your skin till your weariness fades. You will want to touch them, to hold them, to taste them, but they will laugh and push you away, push your face into water, and then begin their games again when you, spluttering, raise your head.

Then they will weave their bodies into a boat and carry you on their backs to the far banks of the river. On its shores they will dress you in a tunic and trousers of the finest muslin. Follow them. Through groves of trees with leaves of green silk, past gardens of flowers carved from glass and jewels. Even the scent of fruit is of amber and musk. But you will not notice this. Not yet.

This is the domain of Turktaz the Beautiful.

Her slavewomen will lead you to Turktaz's bower.

She reclines in a crystal arbour, on a couch of gold draped in brocades.

Her hair is black and her eyes have lights in their darkness like pieces of jade. Her skin is the colour of sunlight cooled in crystal cups of pale wine.

Sit beside me, she will say, in words that echo the dulcimer's notes. Her arms, like jasmine creepers, will enclose you in fragrance. Her limbs are revealed to your gaze by the white gauze of her garments: her flesh gleams through mere veils, held in place by a broad belt of gem-encrusted platinum.

Recline beside her on her brocade couch.

Cupbearers come and go with jewelled decanters of fragrant wine. Her hands will lift jade cups of liquor to your lips. You will taste jasmine and rose and magnolia. Bitter mingling with sweet. Sip gently of these flavours. Keep a hold on your senses. Raise your eyes to her face. Her lips are waiting, open. Kiss her mouth. Taste the rose and the jasmine, the bitter and the sweet. Then look at her breasts, which the fluttering of her hands has half revealed, so you can see their golden globes. Trail your fingers in the valley between. Her hands will play on your chest, on your belly. Now your hands will descend to her belly. You feel the hardness of platinum beneath your fingers. Her loins are encased by the platinum. You search for the buckle of her belt. You fumble with the drawstring of your trousers. Her kisses distract you. Your body is in pieces: your head lost in the joy of her, your thighs gripped by heat and lassitude, your hands, come to life like birds freed from cages, searching, searching.

Her hands will restrain you. Not now, she says. Kiss me all you want. Touch me, smell me, taste me. But don't knock, don't enter. Wait for my body till the seventh night. You'll find the key, then.

Cupbearers come and go with decanters of wine.

She will push you back into a pile of scented cushions. The strange wines have assaulted the workings of your mind. She rises. You tug at her skirt. She laughs. You watch her go.

Cupbearers, their hands empty now, will take her place on the brocade couch. Seven women, each dressed in one colour of the rainbow. They will tickle you and scratch and bite. Their nails at your nipples, their teeth at your thighs. Your hands, made desperate in their urgency and task, will try to pull one of them to you, to complete the unfinished journey you began with Turktaz the Beautiful. But your lassitude makes you their victim. They have their will of you. The hands of one at the drawstring of your trousers, the lips of one taste your mouth, another makes sport with your abject manhood, which, in its unwilling sleep, can still feel the stirrings of a hidden pleasure.

Five nights of this.

Each night you will come to her consumed by the excesses of the night before. Each night her fragrance will revive you. The wine of Turktaz, of her lips, her breasts, her heavy thighs which open a little more, night by night, to your dark and tender probing. Then her laugh and her refusal and her parting back as you, in your drunkennness, lie against the scented cushions and wait for the rainbow women's ministrations.

You will no longer know which passage of joy you have entered or who brings you relief and satiation. You feel your own inner passages invaded by fingers, by tongues, by toys. You can no longer tell when which rainbow-coloured women has made love to you tonight. Each one the shadow-sister of Turktaz. Your closed eyes will see only the features of Turktaz the Beautiful. On the blank screens of your inner lids, the black letters of her name separate and intertwine.

Te, re, kaf, te, aliph, ze.

The vowel curving upward in fifth position reflects your longing.

Then, only one more waiting night.

You think you know now what to do. You cannot bear

another night of this. You will long for the smell of flowers, the taste of fruit, the sight of a leaf falling, dancing on the wind. You will long for the roughness of beer, the sour smell of yoghurt, the soft taste of milk.

You will long for the feeling of flesh on flesh and even more for the joy of flesh enclosed in flesh.

You will long to make Turktaz your possession.

Go again to Turktaz on the sixth night. Recline beside her on her brocade couch. Taste on her lips the jasmine and the rose, the bitter and the sweet. Taste with your tongue the honey trail in the valley between her breasts. Then let your tongue follow the honey trail to her navel. Stroke the heavy velvet of her calves, move upward to the curves of her thighs.

Pour away the wine. Pour it on the satin grass. Spit it into her mouth. But don't let it get to your head.

Cupbearers come and go. You must force her to drink the wine they bring. Turn her wrist, twist her jade cup to her lips. You must say: Give me all tonight, Turktaz. Take all of me. I'm your minion, your slave, your possession. Repay my nights of waiting. I'm sick of sporting with your shadow.

She will push you away. You must insist.

One more night, she says: and then I'm yours.

You have now regained your male strength, your senses. You're prepared to wrestle, to conquer.

You bite her lips.

Your hands assail her breasts.

You rip off her veils.

She will not move.

She has only the protection of her platinum loincloth.

From her right hip hangs the silver key.

Wrest it from its diamond hold. Our strength is in your wrist, in your grasp, the strength of the men in black.

Its lock is between her thighs.

Place the key in its diamond mouth.

Turn.

Taste bliss.

Then fall.

Fall through air, cloud, rain. Sleep if you can: the journey is long, the journey is short. Wake on an islet in the river, half-naked in shredded muslin. Wait for the great bronze bird to take you in its beak. Feel the flames of its eyes. Smell its furnace breath. Come to the stony cloud and rest a moment while the splintered stones gather. Watch them weave themselves into a basket. Step into your vehicle. The eagle drops chains from its beak. Fasten them to the basket before they freeze into stone. Now prepare for your journey.

We are at the gates of the city, awaiting you with newly-woven robes of black. You will not wear them? Did you turn away from the hill, or climb to its peak and tumble down? Or were you one of the chosen who didn't see the basket? Did you wait, perhaps, for the bird to come; did you wait in vain? You were away seven nights. Don't you know the secret? The journey takes place while we tell you our story. The choice is yours: turn back from the hill, or fly to the realm of Turktaz. If you return without seeing her, yours is the road of ordinary men; go back to your cities and your wives, to your chores of earning bread and sweating for milk or beer to moisten the bread.

But if you saw her and tasted her wine, learn the secret of the men in black. The first night with Turktaz and her women is the second, and the second is the fifth, and the sixth night is the first again. No one reaches the seventh night. But in six nights you have learned to live with desire. Your forehead is branded with the name of Turktaz, with the letters of desire. Venture back to the world of contentment and live forever as the outcast you've become. Or return to the rocky hill and wait in vain for the basket and the bird. Or live with us, and wrap yourself in black: it reminds you of the emptiness of longing. Stay with us in our city, where night always rests on the brim of day.

Adiba: A Storyteller's Tale

When the stories had been told, the adults weren't affected, but the children lay in their beds for a long time, thinking. The boys would imagine: I'll grow up to be as brave as the prince, wrestle giants, kill pythons, etc. etc. The girls would think: let my life, too, pass in comfort and luxury like the princess's.

A. R. Khatun, from the preface to *Nur-ul-Ain*

1945

Adiba, alone. She has lived in a grey world since her husband went to the front: suspended for four years (she writes later) between despair and hope. War over, they send her a wire:

YOUR HUSBAND WAS KILLED ON THE
WARFRONT FIGHTING THE JAPANESE IN
MALAYA ON 25 FEBRUARY 1942.

She observes the rituals of mourning – prayers said on the
third day and the fortieth, food distributed to the poor. She
doesn't even know where her husband's grave is, but her grief,
restrained so long, is threatening to spill over. His Majesty's
Government had called up Adiba's husband to fight in 1941.
Though he was way past the age for war, he'd put himself on
the reserve list and asked to be remembered. He'd asked to
go to the Middle East, but they'd sent him to Southeast Asia.
He wrote to her for some months and then she had no more
letters. Only a message that he was reported missing in
Malaya.

She hates the Raj, but that's nothing new; in the thirties,
in those years before the war, they'd said the Imperial sun
was setting, and the women avoided talking to English
memsahibs. Adiba has always advocated freedom from the
British yoke, taking the part of the rebels and the nationalists
even from a distance. But patience is her second name,
perseverance her creed. In her husband's absence she'd started
to write again, at first because she had to, and then she
couldn't stop. They pay her for every instalment she writes.

She needs the money. Her four children are far away, in schools and colleges. A kind publisher from Lahore, who'd admired her first book, came and bought all the copies she had left in store. That helped her, for a while. Then she wrote a new version of a romance she remembered from her childhood, about a brave princess who went out disguised as a soldier lad to rescue her lover from captivity.

Her story came out as a book this year.

The British authorities won't be giving her a pension.

1947

Adiba, alone, makes her choice. She'll migrate, follow the crescent moon, to the new country. It's 1947. The hated British are on the move. Terrible things are happening here – homes and villages set on fire, people herded and chased across the border by armed men who don't ask them whether or not they want to leave. Though she's quite protected, and she isn't afraid, she believes that Delhi is no longer her home: it's time to leave, start a new life. Later, she writes: *The earth of our homeland didn't want us and the sky was saying farewell.*

Her second son is working in a hospital in Lahore. She travels to join him, in a toy plane, carrying what she can in two suitcases and a cloth bundle. She comes to this city by a river, with its bright bazaars, great gold-domed mosque, and many leafy lanes. On its outskirts, there are tombs and a pleasure garden built by a king for his consort.

It's a hard life in this city she's chosen to settle in. She moves from home to temporary home. The first is a cattle shed, a mere store for cakes of buffalo dung. She has two rooms in the next. She hopes or waits for the property the authorities had led her to believe they'd offer her, to compensate for all she's lost. She moves three times in five years. *People who once paid obeisance to your rank now refuse to recognise you. Those who owned a guava tree have claimed an orchard here, and those who owned a brick wall asked for marble mansions.* She isn't young: but she'll spend the next fifteen years writing novels, and fighting for the property she feels the new country owes her to replace what she left behind in the old land.

Many, she sees, are luckier than she has been. She tries to consider the even less fortunate.

1956

Adiba dismisses young writers as anarchists and rebels. Many writers dismiss Adiba as feudal, old-fashioned. *She's a traditionalist,* they say: *She writes in the mode of the past. Her characters are dolls dressed up in finery. Home and hearth suffice for her heroines. She admits she can't speak English.*

She's never read Russian, French or English novels. It isn't modish to write without a purpose or a desire to change the world; to speak of war, strife, oppression and abuse with laughter and irony, as she sometimes does, is considered frivolous. Now righteously indignant young women thirty years younger than she is, eqipped with university degrees, carry off the critical acclaim and the literary prizes. But her publishers press for new work. They tell her she has ten thousand readers a year. Adolescents and housewives can't wait for her novels. A celebrated woman writer comments: *We win the literary awards, she wins the hearts of the young. We're writing of the same matters; but so, so differently.* She tells stories of youths summoned to war by the cruel pale rulers. Of girls who join caravans to cross the new border, escaping mad uncles and careless aunts, to live separated from all they know until rescued from refugee camps. She writes about the brooding young men who pine for these maidens, driven to madness or drink by disappointment and separation. She writes about women whose men fight to free the land from the British, and of the scripture-abusers with long beards who clip youth's wings to try to stop it from soaring. She tells stories of women who bring up their children alone, earning their wages cooking and sewing, or teaching the alphabet and the Holy Book. She writes about the wives of heroes; she writes of heroic wives.

Soldier boys write to her from the front. They ask what

happens later, when the honeymoon's over, to her heroes: Does Shaad's brother marry Azra's cousin? They ask for continuations, sequels, autographs, letters. They tell her, *When we read your stories we find our way home.*

Her daughters, like some of her heroines, graduate. One son becomes a doctor: That way, he says, he can take care of her. She has high blood pressure and a tricky heart.

Critics still make light of her writing. She's a pedlar of romances, a teller of tales. But sometimes, when she looks at new stories, she sees young writers are learning from her, writing about the world she once delighted in painting, but their colours are sombre, and hers layer pastel on bright, like muslin scarves hung out to dry on a line in the sun. Some of the stories could be her own: of betrayal and loss, of the ignominy of men and women. Others sometimes repeat her phrases, the phrases she borrowed so blithely from life, but to different ends. They write about poverty and pain. She says she only wants to give pleasure. She's written about the wars in the world and the struggle for freedom and Pakistan, about borders and partition and the bruises and scars of arrival in a promised land, but that's only the bloody backdrop to stories of hope: she prefers happy endings.

She writes about love.

1960

Alone, as you can be when your children are children no longer
with children of their own, when they still surround you but
remain far away, Adiba grows tired of looking at poverty and
pain. She begins to write romances, tales to read out loud to
her grandchildren. She still says her prayers five times a day.
Though her God hasn't always been good to her she invokes
his blessings on others. She admires the young General who
came to power and will rule the land for the rest of her days.
She remembers him in her prayers.

Her children are always in need, her publishers want her
to write a book a year. But she can't. She treasures her craft,
treasures her time. She continues to love cooking and sewing;
her mind is always on chores and tasks. She makes delicacies
from leftover bread; cuts up a worn-out jacket into patches
for a quilt, stitching purple to orange and scarlet and green,
peacock colours for a cradle or an orphan.

Some critics will say her wonder tales are her life's best
work. They never give her a prize but across the whole land
they call her their teller of tales. She tells the nation its stories:
the stories they've forgotten, the stories they're waiting to
hear.

Each book makes her feel as she felt when the last of her
children was cut out of her womb.

1962 (and 1939)

Adiba, now sixty-two, has been ill for years. Struggling with the novel she feels may be her last, she's rebuilding, again, the homes that have slipped away from her hands, or chasing glimpses of blue mirages before the sun goes down. She writes letters to those journals she once wrote for often, telling readers the stories of her life. She writes about migration and her own woes in the new land: how she was cheated of a property allotted to her by the authorities; robbed of her furniture and chased away by relatives from a house she'd divided and shared.

Sometimes, though, she recalls youth and joy, writes of her days in the old land. Her husband had been an official in the Indian Civil Service. She'd travelled with him from city to city. Each one of her children was born in a different town. She missed the city where she'd come of age and married, but life and her children kept her occupied. She read many books.

One day her husband gave her a story by a friend of his to read, a romance called *Shamim*. She recognised some people in it, and some places. I can do better than this, she thought. She wrote for a month, in secret. Sometimes she snapped at her children, if they pulled at her skirts while she wrote. Her daughter remembers the pencil she used, new when she began, worn out when she came to her story's end. When she'd filled three notebooks, she showed her story to her husband. She'd titled it *Andaleeb*, for the nightingale and her heroine. I'll publish this for you, he said. He chose her pseudonym, Adiba: she was Badar Zamani till then. They were in Delhi. He had a thousand and one copies of her book privately printed, and sent it out to his friends; one was a well-known writer who edited a journal. Her story ran as a serial in eleven instalments. Later, when readers pleaded for more, he would publish a second edition of her book. *Andaleeb: A Tale of Love and Woe* first appeared in 1939. In distant places, the world was preparing its wars. Indian cantonments emptied themselves, one by one, of white men. The war came much closer. And her husband was taken for a soldier.

1965

To the end, young women come to see her, to learn the art of writing romances, but all she can tell them is: *I write what I see and I write from my life.* She doesn't like similes or elaborate figures of speech; her stories have no message, no goal. In writing, as in life, she prefers the middle path. But some of the girls who approach her think her life is her finest piece of work: they come to learn how to live.

People remember a quiet small woman in white, with fragile hands and flesh scarce on her fine bones. Fans often saw her emerge from her kitchen, wiping her hands on her clothes, or they'd find her, shears in hand, dead-heading roses. There are no known photographs.

On the airwaves, from the old country, a woman writer she once met in Delhi, their home town, calls her the last chronicler of a lost world. That's three days before her death. She's still writing.

There'll be a war this September, and the nation will call her favourite general its hero, but she's been gone eight months by then. She won't live to see the worst wars between the old land and the new, or the bloody struggle for the distant east. She's had no regrets about moving. She has missed the old city, but ceased to set her stories there a decade after she landed in the new, because sometimes the light in Lahore reminds her of home, when it falls on a marble floor and picks out the gold of a dome or silvers a pigeon's wing, and here, too, you can smell jasmine and roses and the rain on the breeze, or watch kites – purple and orange and scarlet and green – fly peacock-bright against the horizon. She has found the warm, loud people around her enchanting, though she hasn't been able, so late in her life, to twist her tongue round their words.

But her ancestors knew Lahore. They built a fort here, in which there's a mirrored chamber. A great queen is buried on the outskirts of the city with a poem engraved on her tomb. A dancer, walled alive for belonging to a father and loving his son, gave her name to a district: Pomegranate bud. (Queen and dancer loved the same man, one to exile, the other to death. Both lie in this city, and so does he, the world's conquerer.)

They bury Adiba in this place of intimate strangers. Another woman writer, who'd known her and loved her, washes and shrouds her body for the journey to the grave.

There are many obituaries, on both sides of the border. Many cite *Andaleeb* as her best work; others praise her stories for children. Veterans (some came from the old land) remember:

> Adiba, teller of tales, was born with the twentieth century. She died when she was sixty-five. She came to her new homeland when she was forty-seven. She last saw her husband when she was forty. She gave birth to her first daughter when she was twenty. She married her mother's brother's son when she was nineteen and he was twenty-five. It was a happy marriage.
>
> *Adiba was a descendant of poets and remotely related to the last emperor, the one deposed in 1858 after the First War of Independence, who died in Rangoon, the one who wrote these words:* Father, my home is slipping from my hand, four palanquin bearers are bearing my palanquin away, I'm losing my kin and my strangers.
>
> In 1959, after twelve years in Lahore, Adiba was allotted five rooms in a house. Though she tried to buy the rest of the house from them, her neighbours were litigious and the property remained contested.

1985

Adolescents laid fresh-cut flowers on her grave. Her daughter completed Adiba's last story and went on to write many more books than her mother's six or seven. She never took Adiba's place. People mourned their teller of tales.

Twenty years after her death, a poet exiled to Delhi with only a knapsack says she's carried two of Adiba's books back to her native city. The poet, when she grows tired of the poverty and pain surrounding her, reads Adiba for succour.

She understood pain, the teller of tales. *Hardship*, she wrote, *will be your your best teacher, but never let hardship bring you to your knees*. And she stitched strands of sentences, patterns of phrases, now pastel, now bright, so carefully into the crisp muslin of her pages.

Her best-loved book is about a soldier taken prisoner by the Japanese in World War II. His wife is told he's dead but she doesn't believe the news. But the soldier finds his way home. He's been blinded by the enemy. His wife, in his absence, has given birth to twins. One for each lost eye.

Centenary

Dear Adiba:

This is a tribute on the hundredth anniversary of your birth
from a writer who has spent thirty-one of his forty-six years
in a foreign city. He first read your books seven years ago and
is writing to tell you of the inspiration he draws from your
tales, of the great pleasure they continue to give him. When
he reads you he finds his way home. He asks forgiveness for
playing games with the stories you told, for occasionally re-
ordering the events of your life.

Here is a story he invented in your name. He tells it in
your voice.

A young man who wore a circlet of gold with a ruby that
shone on his brow saved a kingdom from an evil ogre. As a
reward, he claimed the hand of Nilofar, the king's beautiful
youngest daughter. 'Who are you?' the king asked. 'I am Prince
Ahmar', the young man replied. 'My father is the king of a
faraway country, but I have sworn to stay away from my land
for seven years because my brother accused me of a crime I
did not commit, and I am not at liberty to say where I come
from.'

The nuptials took place with pomp and splendour.

Now Nilofar's stepmother and stepsister, who envied her
fortune and her handsome bridegroom, sowed the seeds of

doubt in her heart: Where did the young man come from? To what clan did he belong? But most of all, they wanted the ruby that shone on his brow.

They sent an old courtier disguised as a holy man to tell Nilofar that she must travel on a pilgrimage to a shrine a night's journey away to pray for her bridegroom Prince Ahmar's health and his future. While she was gone they put poppy juice in the golden chalice of milk Ahmar drank from before he slept. Then Nilofar's stepsister crept into the bridal chamber and stole the ruby from the sleeping prince's brow. Ahmar uttered a great cry, and with blood pouring from his nose and his mouth, he fell to the earth and died. But as he fell Nilofar's sister saw the chaplet of gold disintegrate into dust in her hand, and in place of the ruby a tiny drop of blood shone on her palm. Then she heard a great fluttering of wings and she looked up to see, in the darkness, two white birds flying up into the air and out into the night through the wide-open window. Nilofar's stepmother and sister, afraid of the dire consequences of their deed, had Ahmar's body secretly removed and buried in a wild remote place a day and a night's journey away.

When Nilofar returned her stepmother and stepsister told her that her bridegroom was an impostor, an evil trickster. He had stolen her jewels and fled to his land.

But Nilofar didn't believe their lies. She dressed in a suit of clothes Ahmar had left behind, concealed a sharp gold dagger in her bosom, and went out in search of her bridegroom's grave.

Nilofar wandered a day and a night. She encountered many obstacles placed in her way by her sisters. As night fell, she came upon a garden enclosed in marble walls. It was a place of lush green grass and many flowers. A tall cypress tree grew there between two pools of clear blue water. She drank from one pool, washed her hands in another, and then she sat down beneath the cypress tree, her head against its trunk, to rest a while before she resumed her journey. A round gold harvest moon travelled low in the sky.

She was drifting into sleep when she realised she could understand the language of the pair of white birds that softly sang above her head in the tall tree's branches.

'Tell me a tale,' said one of the birds.

'Of what shall I sing, my love?' her mate replied. 'Of my own travels, or of the world's woes?'

'Sing to me of what you have seen in the world today.'

'I will tell you of the prince of a faraway land and his young bride who has been betrayed,' said her mate. So Nilofar heard them tell the whole story of her sister's perfidy, and learned that her husband's life lay in the enchanted ruby she had stolen from his brow.

Then one bird, weeping, said to the other, 'Can the young man never be brought back to life?'

And her mate replied, 'The prince lies within these marble

walls. His garments are the green, green grass and his eyes these pools of blue water. His mouth is a deep red hibiscus. His body is this cypress tree, his hair its green leaves.'

'But if his bride were to catch us, and hold us close, heart to heart, and with one stroke of his sword separate our heads from our necks, so that one of us should not die before the other, and hold our heads above the ground where the prince lies, our blood will spill on the earth and its drops will become rubies more bright than the ruby the wicked woman stole from the prince. Then the prince's heart will beat again in his breast, and he'll return to the land of the living. But if one of us dies before the other, the prince will always lie sleeping.' Nilofar called up to the pair of white birds. They flew down from the high branch and bent their heads before her. 'Soon,' she said to herself, 'I'll see my beloved lying asleep beside me beneath this tree, with a ruby shining on his forehead, and I'll wake him with a kiss on his cheek.'

She took out the sharp golden knife she had hidden in her bosom. Soon the green grass grew red with the blood of white birds.

Turquoise

*Then everything turned blue: the sky, the lake,
the air and the further shore. The universe
became blue. The palace made of clouds now
turned to marble.*

Shafiq-ur-Rahman, 'Neeli Jheel' ('The Blue
Lake')

Nusra came to London in the last year of the century. She
was forty-two. Her life in Islamabad, the city she'd lived in
for nearly a decade, had become empty. Her marriage to a
civil servant was tiresome, her children had grown and flown
to colleges across the sea. She left the NGO she helped to run

in the capable hands of a friend, and took up a scholarship to research a book on contemporary women painters.

She met Danny in winter, at a conference. He was tall for a Javanese, with a receding forehead, a black moustache, and a copper skin. She liked his low voice and his gentle accent. When they ran into each other again on the steps of the college where she was doing her research and he was teaching, Danny suggested they have a cup of coffee. He told her he'd been away.

It was April. It was sunny. They took their paper cups and sat on the stairs. Danny had to leave early, but there was a signal failure on the tube and later he told her he'd arrived at a reception very late.

They met twice a week, once at a seminar they both attended on post-colonial theory, and once, by accident, on the stairs or in the refectory. Accidental meetings became a habit. They never made an appointment. She found out Danny was six years younger than her. He told her he'd been married eleven years. He lived with his wife in Guildford.

Nusra and Danny took to drinking a coffee or two or sometimes a beer on those accidental days, especially when it rained. Nusra wasn't much of a drinker and she didn't like the taste of beer, so once in a way she'd sip wine.

The third week, or was it the fourth, they got very late. Danny was a little tipsy. He worried about keeping his wife waiting, though he said they had a very relaxed relationship.

— I hardly see her these days, he said. She works in an Asian bank and rises before daybreak. She needs her sleep.

Danny missed two of the seminars and when Nusra met him again he said he'd been in Yorkshire and Amsterdam. She didn't ask if he'd gone alone or with his wife. They went for a drink after he'd taught his lesson. Then Danny had another beer and another, and he talked about his life.

— I changed my name from Danarto to Danny and left Surabaya for Yogyakarta when I was nineteen. I sang English songs with a band in a bar because my parents were poor. I sent money home. Then I went to work in a hotel in Bali because the money was better and I spoke good English. I met my wife in Sanur. Her name is Lisa. She was on her way back to London from Australia. She proposed to me in the third week because she was expected in London and she didn't want to leave me behind. It took me several weeks to arrange my papers. I'd always wanted to come to England. I thought I was in love. I wanted to leave Indonesia then, wanted to continue my studies. I'd been in trouble once or twice, street protests and brawls, the army was hard on us. I came here and did the degree I'd always wanted to do at the Slade. Much good it's done me, I hardly get time for my prints. You know I've never talked so much to anyone before.

— As you talked to your wife?

— No. As I talk to you, Danny said.

Then he told her he'd suddenly felt so sick and dizzy the last time he'd gone out with her that he'd fallen off a bus and got a black eye and a twisted ankle. He couldn't remember getting home. He'd woken up on the sitting-room floor and when he looked for his new shoes he couldn't find them.

Nusra and Danny took to having long conversations on the phone in the mornings or afternoons of days they didn't meet. They saw each other three times a week. Weekends were hard for Nusra because Danny went riding in the country with his wife. She'd go to the college on Saturdays and spend a lot of time e-mailing her son in San Diego and her daughter in Atlanta. Once she rang Danny on a Saturday. She found him vague and elusive. She thought his wife must be there.

– This is how it is, for us, Nusra told Danny. I think sometimes I should arrange a seminar for Asian women called 'Nora is alive and well and still living in the doll's house.' I know a woman who paints and dances and teaches, she's a Bangladeshi who lives here, in London. She can't get away for a week without permission from her husband and on the fifth day he can't cope with the kids and is summoning her back. Zuhayr never allowed me to do anything away from home until this year and I lost so many opportunities – in America and Canada and Australia. It's not that I don't like it at home, I do, but I felt I'd done everything I could in

Islamabad, which isn't my city anyway. I was hitting my head against the glass ceiling. When he said I could take up this offer I felt – almost hurt, you understand? As if he didn't need me. Then I guessed he'd been seeing someone else. How hard it is, to leave the doll's house – that's why so many of Ibsen's women commit suicide, and he never tells us where Nora goes.

– Right now I feel I'm in a cage as well, Danny said. Even if you let me out and my wings grow back I'll have forgotten how to fly.

One day Nusra went up to Danny's department to look for him and someone said he'd left for the day. Nusra didn't have anything to do for the next hour so she went down to the cafeteria. Danny found her sitting there a little while later, smoking alone. There'd been a mistake, he said, he was teaching all the time. When they said Nusra had been looking for him he'd gone to the stairwell and shouted her name out so loud they'd had to tell him, You must never do that again, shouting here is against the regulations.

– I can say I love you in your language, Danny told Nusra. *Mujhe tum se pyar hai*. I learnt it from the movies.

One Saturday Nusra was working on a paper she was supposed to write for a seminar but instead she started to write a story. She translated it for Danny when they met on Tuesday. They were sitting in the park.

— It's about a little boy called Danny, she said. He'd been very ill. He was new in town, and while he was getting better he wandered around a lot on his own. There was a lake near his house. One day he met a wild child by that lake. The wild child had blue eyes and wore a string of turquoise beads around his neck. He taught Danny about anthills and flowers from which you could suck honey. He showed him how to impale mating frogs on thorny twigs and catch grass lizards by their tails. One blazing afternoon Danny went to the lake but he didn't find the wild child there. Then he heard a voice calling to him from the water, Come on in. It's cool here and there are pebbles like marbles in the sand at the bottom of the lake. But I can't swim, you know that, Danny said. I'll teach you, the wild child replied. Danny took his hand and stepped into the blue water. He'd never seen so much blue before. Swimming was like flying. And the stones at the bottom of the lake were like the jewels in the Simsim cave. But then the wild child let go of his hand. He was foundering, his mouth full of water, he couldn't breathe, his hands lost their strength, he was falling, falling. And when he woke up, he found himself in his bed again. His father's sticky hand was on his forehead. His mother was saying, We nearly lost you. You've been ill for three weeks. God knows who fished you out of the water. You mustn't ever go near that foul lake again...

– What a beautiful story, Danny said. What happens next?

– I can't say. I haven't finished it yet. But it's for you.

– You've seen through me, then? I'm a sick child alright.

– But you're not the Danny of the story, Nusra said. I'm the one who swam in a lake when I was a child in Karachi and got diphtheria. I guess you're the wild child from the lake.

– No. You're my wild child. And you're also the lake.

– I've been fighting with my wife, Danny said. She's mentioned divorce. I can't afford to live in London on my teacher's salary. I might have to go back to Surabaya. I don't know if I did the right thing, staying here so many years. I should have gone home long ago. Now I feel it might be too late.

He sniffled a little and Nusra shed a tear too. It was June. She laid a hand on his. The sun shone till ten that night. It seemed sinful to be so sad when the sun was shining.

– I might have to move out of the Guildford house, Danny said. It was July. I wonder if you know where I can stay for some days till I get settled.

That night, he came to her house for supper. Nusra made chicken and rice. Danny brought his own red wine. At some very late hour Nusra told him he could sleep on the sofa.

In the morning he'd left for work before she came down. She was having her second cup of coffee when her mother-in-law rang to say that Zuhayr had been taken ill with meningitis. He was alone in Islamabad with no one to take care of him. She didn't have time to talk to Danny before she left. Her daughter flew straight to London and they went back home together.

She made several decisions while her husband got better.

On her way to London Nusra stopped for ten days in Karachi. She put her house, which tenants had just vacated, in order. She was back in London in late September.

She didn't run into Danny till the Christmas celebration. She knew she looked good in her dark winter clothes. She'd pierced her nose at home, and streaked her hair. She crossed the room to say hello.

– I haven't seen you around for a while, she said.

– I took Lisa to see Jogja. Then we flew to Bali. We stayed in Indonesia two months.

Danny looked tired, with very dark lids and shadows below his eyes. He'd grown a beard. He'd had quite a few glasses of wine.

– You didn't answer the e-mails I sent, Nusra said.

– I didn't get them. You could have called.

– My year here's up. I'm going home this month. Zuhayr's coming over to spend the milennium here. Then we'll leave together. We're moving back to Karachi.

– Ring me before you go. We'll have lunch. I'm in a hurry just now. I've got to get back to Guildford. We've got something else on tonight. Lisa's waiting.

Nusra, made bold by one glass of red wine, followed Danny
to where he was checking out his coat and suggested they go
somewhere for a drink.

– Just one, she said. She knew they wouldn't meet again.

– I wanted to tell you the end of that story I wrote, Nusra
told Danny. When the boy who'd been sick rose from his bed
a few days later, a servant handed him a twisted parcel made
of a sheet of old newspaper and tied up with a bit of twine.
The servant said: A beggar boy came to the door. He was
asking for you. I tried to chase him away. He wouldn't leave
until I took this. He insisted there was something in it that
belonged to you. Danny opened the parcel. In it he found the
string of turquoise beads the wild child had worn round his
neck. He went back to the lake many times. In autumn, he
joined a new school. He never saw the wild child again.

Danny and Nusra said goodbye at the bus stop in December
sleet.

The Needlewoman's Calendar

*Husnara said: 'Mistress, colours for the rainy
season: red, orange, pomegranate-blossom,
peach-blossom, melon colour, rice-green,
maroon; and for the winter: marigold colour,
yellow ochre, crimson, grass green, dusky
brown, purple, black, dark blue, rose colour,
saffron, slate colour, light brown; and for the
hot weather: light green, steel colour, campak-
colour, cotton-flower colour, almond colour,
camphor white, milk white, poppy-seed
colour, falsa-colour, sandal wood colour, and
bright red. And there are plenty of other
colours beside these...'*

Nazir Ahmad, from *The Bride's Mirror*, 1869,
translated by G. E. Ward, 1903

1

Tabinda was embroidering orange flowers on a bedspread for the trousseau of her youngest sister-in-law when suddenly she knew what she would do.

Thoughts had been ravelling and unravelling in her hands since she'd heard the news that her absent husband had come back from London with Charity Bunce, his landlady's daughter. They were now in Rawalpindi, living many miles away from the shadow of his parents' ire. In the family conference that had followed the arrival of his letter, her father-in-law informed her that she would, of course, stay on in the family home in Lahore, afforded all the privileges of the first and official wife, and when her husband visited once or twice a year he, too, would treat her as he should a first and treasured wife. She had begged to be sent home to her parents, at least for a while: but her mother-in-law couldn't bear the thought of losing face, and forbade her to leave. But since Tabinda had heard the news she'd been a captive of corners, hiding her face from the light. Her heavy earrings weighed her down, and when she heard the jangling of the bracelets on her wrists she trembled.

She was sewing on the terrace, in the cool evening air, and with each stitch she reflected on her situation. Two boys were flying a kite from the roof of the house next door. On the watchman's radio, a woman sang, in a deep sweet voice, of a maiden weaving garlands while she waited for her beloved: *I'll wear black and won't take a comb to my hair till I hear the sound of your returning footsteps, I'll cling to your feet when you enter my garden and implore you not to leave.* But Tabinda hadn't been waiting for her husband with rapture of this kind, only a faint fear: she had never known rapture at all. She'd felt only despair when they dressed her in red, braided her hair and covered her face with flowers on her wedding day and then put her in the palanquin – actually a Bentley, festooned with flowers for the occasion – that took her to her bridegroom's home. Despair had faded to resignation when, day after day, she'd sit alone with her needle and night after night submit to his needs in the marital bed. Her husband Suhayl was a distant relation she'd always disliked: but his mother, her mother's cousin and 'sister by affection', had chosen her because she was a simple, well-trained girl of impeccable Shaikh lineage, whose family traced descent from a saint. She was the most likely candidate to give the family the male heir they required before Suhayl left to continue his legal studies abroad. But Suhayl went back to England after seven weeks. She knew a little later she was carrying his child. She longed for her mother but stayed on in the family mansion with its many rooms and leafy garden. They watched her, cosseted her, fed her fruit and nuts and milky sweets until, in blood and anguish, she gave birth to the daughter they didn't want. Their disappointment was evident. But never mind, they said, she was young and so was her husband — he'd be back in three years, then there'd be time. But soon the unwelcomed girl child, whom she'd given the name of Nasreen, awakened a love within her as fierce as a swarm of honey bees. Her in-laws had soon become aware of her prowess with the needle and between the moments she spent with her child, or in prayer, and the many spare hours in which she'd sew anything that was required in the house, the months and then the years had gone by, and if there was no bliss in this home so far from her own there was at least, for a girl who'd come from a needy family, the semblance of tranquillity.

If she'd been afraid of Suhayl's return, she was even more afraid of staying on in this house without him now. Since she'd heard he had a new wife she'd been thinking of an old, old story.

A prince lay in an enchanted garden with needles covering him from the crown of his head to the soles of his feet. A banished princess came upon him and set herself the task of removing the needles one by one. But when only the needles of his eyes remained she left him sleeping and went to the river to bathe. When she returned she found the last of the needles in the hand of her servant woman who claimed to be the prince's true bride.

And Charity, plump-cheeked and blonde, whose photograph Tabinda had once found in the pocket of a jacket

Suhayl left behind, was the one who had removed the last of the needles from Tabinda's husband's eyes. Contrary to what the proverb derived from the story implied, removing needles from such sensitive tissue was a painstaking task: didn't Charity, then, deserve the prize – for who, in the circumstances, was the true bride? And had Suhayl ever been much more to Tabinda than a stranger? Let Charity keep him, Tabinda decided. The needle in her hand, which she hadn't extracted from any part of her husband's being, would be her means of future living.

2

Tabinda had been planning her escape. She gathered a few – only a few – of the jewels she'd been given by her in-laws, which she felt she deserved in lieu of the alimony she was unlikely to receive, and tied them up in a square of brightly-chequered silk. She dressed up her daughter, pulled on her own white burqa over the light clothes she was wearing, and left a message for her mother-in-law, who was downstairs playing cards, saying she was going out to the family jewellers' with a broken string of pearls and an earring to repair. She sent the gatekeeper to fetch a tonga to take her to the centre of town.

The jeweller she visited, who was used to the women of

her family coming to him to buy and not to sell, was astonished when she sold him two heavy gold bracelets and a gem-encrusted wedding ring for only a little more than the price of a train ticket from Lahore to Karachi. If her mother-in-law followed her trail and wanted to retrieve the lost jewels, the jeweller, she thought, could always sell them back to her.

To save money, she travelled third class. There were only women in the compartment, and most of them, like her, wore the veil in public spaces. But she was aware that, for the first time ever, she was out in the world, alone, unprotected. She held little Nasreen close to her all the way. The child was often hungry, and she bought some snacks to allay her hunger – chickpeas, potatoes, fried bread and, for herself, milky tea.

After a journey of a day and a night, she arrived at Karachi's cavernous and chaotic station. She left her burqa behind on the seat of the compartment she was vacating, in a pile of greying white. She took Nasreen's hands and walked out into the city. Her thin lilac dopatta was hardly large enough to cover her head and shoulders, and her satin clothes clung to her limbs in the heat. She draped the dopatta over her bosom, pulling one end over the crown of her head. She would never cover her face again.

If the passage from Lahore was frightening, the journey through Karachi in a rickshaw with the sea breeze grazing her bare cheek was worse. But it was exhilarating as well. She remembered with affection the little house in Lalukhet which she'd seen only once when she went home to have her baby there, with its lime-daubed walls and the uncarpeted floor which her mother washed every morning with bucket upon bucket of precious water so that it was rarely dry and the rooms remained cool. It was, though small, better than the shack she'd lived in for a few months when her family first reached Karachi, which was the home she'd been sent away from as a bride. She thought of her father, who was always reading the Quran in search of answers to the knotty problems of the day, and of her mother whose greatest pleasure and luxury was the acquisition of white sugar on her ration card to cook halwas of carrot and pumpkin and semolina. She thought of her brother who, as a youth, sat up night after night in a public garden to study for his Munshi Fazil exam in the electric glow of a streetlamp so that he didn't deplete their house's supply of light, and of her sister-in-law whose feet, the last time she saw her, were heavy with the child she was carrying, the little boy Tabinda had never seen, who must be three years old now. She passed the swamps where black buffaloes lolled, and little settlements of shacks and lean-tos, and then she saw and and smelt the dusty squares and lanes of Lalukhet. She heard the muezzin's voice fill the neighbourhood: she'd reach home in time for the evening prayer.

3

Though Tabinda hadn't had time to tell her family she was coming home, she knew that after a period of distress akin to mourning, caused by their daughter's misfortune, they'd regain their good sense.

As they did. Tabinda's mother railed against all benighted men like Suhayl who fell victim to the spells and blandishments of Vilayati trollops.

– Those *mems*, she muttered. They cling to our poor boys like leeches. Aren't their own men good enough? They eat pig's meat for breakfast. How can angels visit their houses? They wear knee-length frocks with tiny drawers like *this* beneath, and wipe off the soil and secretions of their nether parts with squares of paper. Then they bathe themselves in still water, soaking in their own filth. Then they let their puppies sleep in their bed and lick their faces. How, I ask you, can the angels of mercy set foot in houses such as theirs? They look like boiled turnips with glass marbles for eyes and straw for hair. There was a lady doctor from the mission nearby who used to visit us in Bhopal – a kind woman, poor soul, I must admit – but my mother would cover the chair she sat on with a white sheet she kept especially for 'mem' visitors so we wouldn't have to sit where their bottoms had been.

Tabinda's brother, as her advocate, wrote to her in-laws,

asking for a divorce. Shaikh Usman Hanafi, Tabinda's father, had consulted the religious books and all the reformist laws derived from them.

– If you allow Suhayl to divorce you, he told Tabinda, you can justifiably claim the substantial alimony pledged to you in the marriage contract.

But Tabinda remained adamant.

– I want to divorce Suhayl. He's observed none of the conditions that allow him a second wife. He hasn't asked my permission to remarry. I'm not barren or deranged. He won't be dividing his time fairly and equally between his new wife and me.

Tabinda's advocates didn't demand alimony, but they wanted custody of Nasreen, who in any case was an infant and far below the age of seven at which a child may choose between her parents. She must be kept by her mother. Tabinda's father was quite sure, though, that a girl child would be of little concern to her husband's parents. And Tabinda, though she would never have spoken of it, knew that she may be betraying her parent-in-laws' hopes for a reconciliation and a male heir born of a thoroughbred mother, but she was also freeing the man who had shared her life for forty-nine nights from his obligations to her. And the straw-haired bride who removed the last needle from his eye would finally breathe the air of freedom and relief.

4

There remained, of course, the question of subsistence. How could she drain the meagre resources of parents who, from their misguided love of her, had chosen a husband who was to have provided her, far away from the home of her girlhood, all the comforts they had been denied in their lives?

Her brother was a petty clerk in a government office. Her father, who before he came here had been a schoolteacher, had no pension, though he still supplemented the family income by taking in students from the neighbourhood to whom, in spite of the cataracts now clouding both his eyes, he taught the words and cadences of the Holy Book.

Tabinda, too, could recite by heart every word of the Quran. And she knew its meaning, too. Should she go out and teach its message to little girls? But the role of an ambulant teacher of scriptures wasn't one to which the gently nurtured women of her family were suited. And the older boys who came to study with her father would never willingly countenance the guidance of a young woman.

But then she had known, for a long time, the professional pursuit she'd ultimately choose. She'd take in the neighbours' sewing.

Soon, she was preparing an entire trousseaux. She embroidered napkins, tablecloths, bedspreads for the wives of the better-off. She stitched sequins on scarves for brides, and knitted pullovers to keep babies warm in mild Karachi winters.

Her mother protested.

– Did we bring you up for work like this? Who thought my daughter would become a seamstress? Think of the loss of dignity! No woman in our community has ever soiled her hands like this before, touching other people's garments! I dreamed that all you'd do in your husband's home was sit on a silver chair and sleep in a bed of flowers...

In response, Tabinda quoted an example from the *Bahishti Zevar* she'd been given as a bride to carry with her Quran:

– Didn't Zainab bint Jahash, the Holy Prophet's wife, work with her hands and didn't our Messenger himself praise her for the generosity of her 'long hands'?

And her father, from the corner near the window where he was smoking his hookah in the winter light, added:

– And the redoubtable author of the *Bahishti Zevar* himself recommends that virtuous women follow in that illustrious lady's footsteps and take in work to keep their idle hands busy at home. Calligraphy, bookbinding, teaching the alphabet, sewing and the making of pickles are all lucrative occupations suited to the wives and daughters of the virtuous.

When the work at hand became too much for her to deal with on her own, Tabinda asked her father for the use of the covered veranda in which he had taught his students who, one by one, were drifting politely away. She hired three women from the neighbourhood to come in and help her with the work.

One day a woman drove up in a shining new car and asked to see her.

– The woman who looks after my children lives in this neighbourhood and told me about you, she said. I believe you do *zardozi*? I want this jacket embroidered for my daughter's *bismillah*.

– Anything you want, Tabinda said. She went to work.

Other affluent clients followed. Soon the house was full of baskets of thread, bolts of cloth and lengths of fine fabric in varying stages of readiness. Tabinda sensed her sister-in-law's unease at their over-crowded quarters.

But once again Tabinda's keen eye helped her out of the situation she found herself in. A seamstress who worked with her told her of a small warehouse nearby that was lying empty. She covered her head and shoulders with a grey shawl and went off to bargain with its owner for a fair rent.

Within a week, she had supplied the scrubbed single room with a modicum of furniture – chairs, stools, sewing machines, pitchers for cool water, even a small stove to make tea. It travelled across the neighbourhood in a camel-cart. In the month after Ramadan she moved her seamstresses, along with an ageing machinist who had now joined them, and his small grandson to whom he was teaching the craft, into her new shop.

A poster, proclaiming *NAUBAHAR: Ladies' and Childrens' Garments and Fancy Needlework* in bright green letters, hung resplendently above the door.

5

Five years after her return to Karachi, Tabinda was able to rent a tiny plum-coloured building on the fringes of the expanding district of P.E.C.H.S., to which she moved her workshop and showroom. The disused servants' quarter of a bigger house which had been rented to American missionaries who didn't need rooms for servants, it had been found for her by their cook, who knew the husband of one of the seamstresses from Lalukhet.

The house had a wall festooned with the purplish bougainvillea that grew so profusely in this neighbourhood, and a low wooden back gate she used as a separate entrance. The fine folk of the city who availed themselves of her skills had found Lalukhet too distant for their chauffeurs to drive them to, but the prices they were ready to pay for the fine traditional embroidery they demanded had enabled Tabinda to change her location. She left the machinist, his grandson, and three women who didn't want to work away from Lalukhet in charge of the old shop. In the new premises, there was almost too much work: Tabinda had to hire many more hands, among them a number of residents of the nearby refuge for destitute women, who took home two-thirds of the price Tabinda charged customers for their work. Two years ago, when she'd sent the sum she received for the bracelets and the ring she'd sold back to her parents-in-law, a money order for a substantial amount had come from them in lieu of a receipt, to help, she supposed, with the expenses of Nasreen's upkeep. She'd cashed it and banked the sum in an account she opened in Nasreen's name. Thinking of the plight in which she'd have found herself if she hadn't had her parents to support her, and her own faith and enterprise to see her through, she now set aside a part of her income in a charitable trust for abandoned women and their offspring. One Friday a month, after prayers, she fed the poor of the neighbourhood in her courtyard.

Soon Naubahar was known as the best shop of its kind.

6

A teacher from the girls' school nearby took to dropping

Nasreen at her mother's shop after classes. On the pretext of having an outfit stitched for Eid, she befriended Tabinda. Her name was Shamim. A lively, talkative graduate with a degree in education, Shamim had bobbed, permed hair and, in her mid-twenties, was in no hurry to marry. In the afternoon, she sipped tea and nibbled savoury snacks with Tabinda who, with much of the heavier work now delegated to her staff, had a little time to spare.

Shamim asked Tabinda for a signed photograph one day. Some days later, she handed her a slim volume of verse. It was, she said, written by her brother, Omar Baig.

Tabinda had, until now, found no time to make friends. But with her daughter at school she was sometimes lonely. These days, with Shamim's visits, she had company. A rare source of entertainment over the year or so since she'd started to work in P.E.C.H.S. was a trip to Elphinstone Street, where she shopped among the society ladies and the foreigners, or to Saddar for fabric or shoes, or a visit to the neighbouring Khayyam cinema with Nasreen. But in all these years she hadn't walked on the Clifton esplanade or in Frere Hall's gardens, or seen the Zoo.

Six years had passed since her divorce, and she hadn't seen her former husband for nearly ten. At times she wondered about that callous stranger she married who had never wanted to know his own daughter, and the straw-haired *mem* he'd brought across the sea to Pakistan. How were they faring?

Had they moved back to Lahore or did they live in London? Was he now the father of that son and heir her parents-in-law had acquired Tabinda to produce? Sometimes she felt as if she had been enchanted since her divorce, like those princesses who slept in a spell all day and only rose at night, except that it was at night, when she heard the peaceful breathing of her family through the thin walls around her, that she felt forgotten and lonely.

Nasreen was nine, and Tabinda nearing thirty. She'd been independent for a while and, though she rose before dawn to make the journey by rickshaw to drop Nasreen at school before opening the shop, and still travelled back every evening to her parent's little home to sleep there with Nasreen beside her on a mattress, she had furnished a room with a bed for herself in the house she rented, and there was also a bigger room for Nasreen. The child, who'd never had a room of her own to sleep or dress in, used it with joy in the evening, before her mother took her back by rickshaw, soon after sunset, to Lalukhet. She brought schoolfriends here, with whom she'd do her homework in her room, or play in the yard that lay between her house and the missionaries'. Brought up with her boy cousin, Nasreen was now, in the company of her schoolfriends and in the long hours she spent in the house in PECHS, growing unused to Lalukhet. She really only saw her family at weekends, when her cousin was out playing ball on the streets with his playmates, and all she could do there was spend her time reading, drawing animals or playing with her dolls alone.

Tabinda often secretly considered shifting with Nasreen into the rooms she had furnished. Her brother's family was growing, and they could do with the added space her departure would allow. He'd been offered, as a government servant, a house in the nicer district of Nazimabad, in which he could make a new home for his family. Tabinda knew there'd be no room in this new life for her. He had, in fact, offered more than once to arrange a government loan for her, to enable her to buy the property she rented.

– You should remarry, her sister-in-law said frequently. There are widowers who would be happy to acquire a wife with an income of her own, and as for Nasreen – well, what with your position in the world as a woman of considerable means, you can always send her to boarding school in Murree. Or else you could stay on here with Abbajan and Ammi – but people would talk. You're fine as long as you have your brother's hand of protection on your head, but if we leave you alone here with them – a single woman who works – people will talk.

But Tabinda had never dreamed of a second marriage. After the unedifying experiences her body and then her mind had undergone with Suhayl, she wouldn't consider the notion of sharing her life with a man she didn't know. Discreet proposals had been brought to her father's doorstep, but she always suspected that the men who asked for her hand wanted a nanny for their children, or knew about her financial security. She had heard stories of men who, though they had no legal right over their wives' assets, had, through various machinations, drained rich girls of everything they brought with them. She could, she thought, move her parents with her into the new house. But there was hardly room for them there and they wouldn't, at their age, want to leave their son and grandson to move so far away. And telling them she was leaving their home to live alone? It would break their hearts. The question didn't arise.

For years Tabinda had been embroidering, on a bedspread, a tree with bright birds on its spreading branches. A blue and gold stream flowed beside it, from which two golden does were drinking. It's for Nasreen's wedding, she told herself.

7

Tabinda was waiting alone in the mild March afternoon for Shamim to bring Nasreen home. She idly watched a blue-winged bird shake water-beads off its wings and wondered where it had taken a dip. From the cinema nearby she could hear Noorjehan's plaintive voice:

Chand hanse, duniya base, roye mera pyaar re
Dard bhare dil ke mere toot gaye taar.

Earlier, instead of the religious pamphlets or the women's digests she usually read, or the amber beads she told in spare moments, Tabinda had picked up from her table the volume of verse Shamim had left with her. A sketch of the poet, whose pseudonym was Armaan, graced the book's jacket. She noted a fine wide forehead, deep intelligent eyes, thin lips and a firm jaw.

Two verses captured her restless eye. One spoke of the seasons: How, the poet asked, could those who suffered winter's winds ever forget the smell of the jasmine in spring? The other celebrated the blue of the sea. Above the second poem, someone had written: *To those dark eyes that have never seen the blue sky look at its reflection in the sea's waves.*

Shamim had told Tabinda once that her brother took her to Clifton sometimes on the back of his scooter, and Tabinda remembered saying: In all the years I've been back in Karachi, I've only twice, and very briefly, seen the sea. She realised that Shamim must have passed the information on – with some amusement – to her brother.

Sipping tea with Shamim later, Tabinda, carefully and casually, once again brought up her wish to see the sea. Shamim suggested a trip to the beach that Sunday. Her brother would drive them there in a borrowed car.

8

— I don't know how much Shamim has told you about me, Omar said to Tabinda at the beach while Shamim and Nasreen rode on camels' backs. I work for the Urdu newspaper *Naya Zamana* and scribble verses in leisure moments. My dream is to own a bookshop. I'm twenty-seven. I came alone to Karachi when I was seventeen. I still live in the family home in Bahadurabad, where we've been since my parents came to Karachi from the Deccan seven years ago, in '51. I favour progressive politics and I don't mind the occasional drink, but I fast, and never fail to go to the mosque on Fridays. I decided (he continued quite hesitantly), if you don't mind mind my saying this but I'd rather say it all to you myself, that you were the right person for me even before I saw the autographed photograph Shamim took from you to show me. I want to ask you first, before I take any steps, if you have any objection to my parents visiting yours...

I'm a divorced woman with a daughter, Tabinda wanted to tell him, but that seemed redundant because he must already be aware of her past, as her daughter was right there with them. Neither could she find words to say she'd let him know. She didn't speak. And then, to break the silence, she said:

— The sea in poems and songs is always blue. But in this light, wouldn't you say, it's the colour of a turquoise.

9

Though it seemed incongruous, particularly because Tabinda was a divorced woman and Omar a younger man, Shamim's parents came to Lalukhet with gifts and a formal request for Tabinda's hand. They were doubtful at first because of the difference in age and the knowledge of her failed first marriage, but, Shamim told her later, her mother had taken one look at the modest bespectacled young woman who hardly ever raised her eyes to them and had been persuaded. Tabinda's entrepreneurial reputation probably helped.

Tabinda and Omar were married in June. They'd known each other since March. Only the two families attended the wedding. Tabinda hadn't wanted to dress up, but Shamim draped her in a red chiffon sari, and put a string of jasmine, punctuated with a single rose, in her long hair. Now take off your spectacles! Shamim said. Tabinda didn't like jewellery, but her mother-in law had given her earrings and bracelets she'd worn at her own wedding, and Tabinda had to wear those, though she drew the line at the sprinkling of powdered gold on her face and hair.

Omar's part of the wedding contract stipulated, on his insistence, a *meher* of twenty-five thousand rupees. Tabinda's one condition for marriage was that Omar should move with her into the rooms she'd furnished in her rented house. Nasreen, until she chose to do so, was never to leave them. Yes, and Omar was never, ever to touch strong drink.

10

Slowly, subtly, life was changing. Even though most of the work was done by her staff, Tabinda still did the fine embroidery for which she was much in demand and rarely put her needle down before the evening's prayer. Omar usually came home even later, an hour or two after sunset. But now in the evenings, after Nasreen had gone to bed, they would sit together in a part of the long corridor Tabinda called the gallery, where she'd arranged chairs, a divan and a low table for their leisure moments. Tabinda, who'd always been unused to talking, listened to Omar's stories of the day, particularly about Ayub's government, of which she had no particular opinion and he didn't approve. Tabinda learned new terms: 'guided democracy', 'free speech', 'the abrogation of civil liberties'. Omar read out the editorials he was drafting for the following day, in which he took on everything from the adulteration of milk and the price of petrol to the lack of proper schools in the deprived section of the city and the resulting illiteracy of children forced to work at ridiculously early ages. Tabinda also found herself talking: at first about accounts and Nasreen's future, and then about matters of faith, which Omar, like she did, saw in the same light as the need for food and housing, since both were realities of day-to-day living.

Sometimes Omar's friends, poets and painters and journalists, came over on a Saturday evening. They sat and talked, among bolts of cloth and unfinished garments, drinking numerous cups of tea and smoking cigarettes until day broke. Omar asked Tabinda to join them and sometimes she stayed to listen to a new poem. But mostly she smiled, greeted them and slipped away.

Once or twice, Omar had taken Tabinda to an all-night performance by a troupe of renowned *qawwals* who'd also migrated from the Deccan. And she enjoyed their singing so much she decided, I'll ask Omar to invite them to perform at our house, one day.

At night, Tabinda's dreams made mischief: now she waded knee-deep in a ditch filled with rainwater, now she was slapping and moulding wet mud into cakes. She was up a tree eating a raw, stolen guava, or squatting in the grass with a slice of water melon in her hand, its illicit red juice dripping off her chin. She'd open her eyes in the mellow dark and Omar's head beside her on the pillow was comfortable. And – she dared to admit it – comforting.

11

It rarely rained in Karachi, but this year there was lightning and water came down in sheets of silver needles. In the rain-filled ditches buffaloes reclined, still as tombstones. The streets were flooded and the courtyard of Tabinda's house had become a pond. Tabinda, after forbidding Nasreen to play in the first downpour's vapours, actually found herself enjoying the rivulets lapping at her bared ankles when she ran out to pull Nasreen indoors.

The rain hadn't paused for breath that Friday afternoon. It was drumming alien songs on tin roofs, turning flower beds into pools, ditches into boating basins. Tabinda heard the unlocked door swing open and thought it was Omar coming home early after prayers as he often did on a Friday. But instead she saw two uniformed policemen stride into the house. They ransacked the room in which she and Omar slept, turned the papers on Omar's desk upside down and flung papers on the rug from his drawers, but they didn't find what they seemed to be searching for, and they left in a rage, without answering Tabinda's stammering questions.

Omar didn't come home that night. And Tabinda, for the first time since their wedding, was afraid. In the ten months they'd been married she hadn't spent a single night alone and now doors and windows banged open and shut all night in the storm wind. Tabinda thought of taking Nasreen, whom she'd told that Omar was away on work, to Bahadurabad, but she didn't want to frighten Omar's parents. And she told Shamim, too, to pretend that Omar was away on a job in Sukkur if they asked for him.

Her feet were heavy now, very heavy. Nasreen had been a light burden, but with this coming one she finally understood the meaning of the expression. She had almost no appetite and still, at the oddest moments, she'd throw up the little she did eat.

Omar hadn't come home for twenty-nine days and Tabinda didn't know what to do. She couldn't call the police because she knew they were involved. Ashraf, the editor of the newspaper Omar worked for, had come to tell her how policemen had walked in and frog-marched Omar away from the office. There'd been a crowd outside the American embassy, and a few stones pitched at a minister's passing car, and both events linked to Omar's Op Eds, and then after Friday prayers one day Omar was spotted in a mob of protesters... Ashraf and his friends were working on Omar's release.

– I'll stand bail if required, Tabinda told Ashraf in the second week, when, head covered with customary grey shawl, she went to meet him in the office near Kutchery Road. Even to the extent of mortgaging my assets.

– That may not be necessary, was Ashraf's response. But a wad of crisp notes in the right hand...

Tabinda vowed that if Omar came home safely – *when* Omar came home safely – she'd feed the poor two Fridays a month. No, every Friday. In the evenings she kept her hands busy by working on the bedspread she worked on in leisure moments. Recently, since Omar and she had made a home, she hadn't had time for such painstaking stitches.

But she worked every rain-coloured day with red and green and gold threads till her fingers were tired and her eyes watered behind their spectacles. She'd cover their bed with it on the day Omar came home. She brightened the wings of the birds and the petals of the flowers. On the borders of the bedspread she embroidered Omar's verse about the winds of winter and the jasmine in spring. But I should, she thought as she stitched, make something to shield us from the winter wind. Decembers can bring a chill blast from the desert.

Nasreen tugged at her sleeve and said, Someone is calling your name. Tabinda, thinking it was only the storm, unlatched the door for a rain-drenched Omar. Outside, the wind was whipping leaves off trees. Omar's head was shaved, he had an arm in a sling, and a purpling bruise on his cheekbone. His smile revealed a broken tooth. He'd been away thirty nights.

When he'd bathed and changed into clean clothes, Omar slumped down in his usual chair with a cup of tea on the low table in front of him and a cigarette in his hand.

– They hauled me off to Hyderabad jail, he said to the percussion of the rain on the window. They interrogated me for hours every day. What processions had I walked with, which demonstrations had I been part of, who did I know, did I receive publications from the Russian embassy or read communist propaganda, did I believe in the word of God, why did I write such fiery editorials and what did I mean by the constant references to winter and spring in my poems – do I intend a change of government or regime? In spite of the slaps and kicks they gave me, I said: I fast and I pray like the next good man and as a Muslim I know I have the God-given right to protest against unjust rulers. But I believe in solving problems with pen and ink, not sticks and stones. My poems, if you bother to read them properly, are always and only about love. By the way, I haven't been married for long. That's a good subject for my poems and marriage takes up a lot of a man's time, it keeps him off the streets. That bit of cheek earned me the punch in the mouth that broke my tooth.

They'd let him go home, with a stern warning not to write any more incendiary articles or poems. He'd had to ride rough to get home, with the few rupees he had left in his pocket. He thought that it was someone at his paper, who knew someone high up in the police, who'd got him off so easily this time. Tabinda didn't mention her meeting with Ashraf.

That night, Tabinda covered their bed with the bright silk spread she'd just finished embroidering.

– Touba, the tree in the paradise garden, Omar said when he saw it. I always said you were a painter with your needle.

Later, when he lay down again after switching off the light, Tabinda told Omar:

– If you want to leave your job that's fine, you can stay at home and write poetry till the dust settles. Or you can start your bookshop nearby.

Then she said she was carrying his child, but she hadn't told anyone yet, not even Shamim. Omar said he hoped it would be a little girl who was as pretty as Nasreen and her mother. But a boy would be welcome too. The baby was coming in April and, though she has never mentioned her wish to him, Omar said: I'll call the Hyderabadi *qawwals* to perform here when the child arrives. Then he slid down in the darkness and put his head against Tabinda's belly, to listen for heartbeats, he said. She laughed out long and loud for the first time in years and tousled his hair.

– Don't be such a fool, she said. It's still too early for the baby to make a sound.

12

Storms had washed away the shacks and lean-tos that people who'd once been refugees in the settlements on the city's edges had been living in for more than a decade. Omar, though he'd sworn to his editor and his parents and his wife that he'd keep the flames out of his verses and his prose for a while, was petitioning the municipality to reconstruct the settlements with mortar and bricks. But nothing was happening in spite of promises and you could see people on the way to Lalukhet scurrying about like ants with baskets on their heads or backs. They were rebuilding their fallen homes.

Shamim still brought Nasreen home from school every day, and lingered for a cup of tea amd a chat before Omar came in. Omar insisted that Nasreen, obsessed as she was these days with insects, lizards and frogs, would grow up to become some kind of scientist. Shamim, in preparation, had taken the child's education in hand. Since she learnt Tabinda was going to give her a brother or sister Nasreen had started to call Omar 'Abbu'. Her logic told her that her brother or sister's father had to be her father too.

Omar had seen an empty stall in the market they called

the Nursery just nearby, in which he wanted to open his bookshop. He'd also found a car, a battered Opel, that a garage-owning friend of his wanted to be rid of and was selling cheaply. He'd wanted to buy it with the money his father had given him when he married, but Tabinda insisted on sharing the cost, as she could now travel in ease to Lalukhet.

Green velvet spread over the city of dust and rocks after the five rainy weeks. People wanted gardens: everywhere they were planting red and yellow flowers, and growing trees. Even the poorer quarters were festooned with bright bougainvillea. Tabinda, feasting her eyes on the gulmohar and the green branches in which parrots and mynahs nested, would try to recollect the name of that poet who'd once said that paradise was right here, in this world.

On weekends Tabinda and Omar would drive to the leafy suburb where his parents lived with Shamim, who hadn't yet any plans to marry. Or they'd visit her family in the dustier part of the city. Tabinda's parents, now that their children were settled, were planning, after all these years, to make the pilgrimage to Mecca.

Sometimes Tabinda and Omar would go for hot chocolate and cakes to the Portuguese cafe near the cathedral in Sadar, or they'd eat biryani in the car near Jinnah's tomb and he'd tease her for putting morsels in her mouth with a spoon instead of a fork.

– But I've always eaten rice with my fingers, Tabinda would say with a laugh.

And sometimes Omar picked up their relatives and drove them over to P.E.C.H.S., where they ate kebabs that Omar, on his way home from his office, had bought at Bundoo Khan's on Bunder Road. I've forgotten how to cook, Tabinda would say. And Omar – well, Omar in the kitchen was a laughing matter.

Sometimes on the drive back at night from Lalukhet to P.E.C.H.S. they'd fall silent, and Tabinda's eyes would follow the moon through the open window, the late breeze on her face reminding her of the day she travelled all the way back to Karachi from Lahore, when she'd been so afraid even though she was all wrapped up in her stifling white burqa, and after that she'd hardly stepped out anywhere for pleasure, and the months turned into years and lurched across the sandy pages of the earth like a line of twelve great camels on its way to the sea, till that March afternoon had brought her riding on its back to the place where the light skimmed the turquoise waves, that place on the shore of the world where she'd looked out from under her eyelashes and the steady gaze that met her own was bright with time, and even before he said a word she knew Omar was the one who'd brought the fiery seasons she'd waited for to rouse her from her dreamless winter, this man who didn't need her helping hand to pluck the needles from his body or his eyes, because if he'd ever had them there he'd shed them, one by one, and he'd been wide awake for a long, long time.

Acknowledgements

Two of these stories have been published before: 'Cactus Town' in *Tank*, and 'The City of Longing' in *The Virago Book of Erotic Myths and Legends*. I'd like to thank Malu Halassa of *Tank*, and my sister Shahrukh Husain Shackle for commissioning a story which made me turn to Nizami's *Haft Paikar* for inspiration.

Thanks also to:
Peter Middleton and Sujala Singh (at the University of Southampton where I began writing these stories while I held a Southern Arts Writing Fellowship in Spring 2000), for their encouragement and continuing interest. At Saqi Books, Mai Ghoussoub for her involvement with these stories from start to finish, some tough criticisms and heated discussion, and even more for a decade of friendship; Sarah al-Hamad for inspiring me throughout; and André and Salwa Gaspard for their initiative and flair. At home, my mother, for her encyclopedic knowledge of matters cultural, linguistic and

religious, and my nephew Roman, who read and approved of the first few stories. Among my friends, Hanan and Kamila, and above all Mimi Khalvati, whose unstinting affection and belief in me have made writing these stories a greater pleasure as I always anticipate her laughter and frowns as she reads by her window in Evering Road. Last but not least Uma Waide, my lifelong friend, for reading the manuscript with a diligent and critical eye.

For those who care about such things, the excerpts from Urdu are translated by me except where mentioned. The stories are arranged in the order of their writing, but can be read in any sequence the reader chooses.

Aamer Hussein
London 28 April 2002